Summer Sizzle

by

Samantha Gentry

Summer Sizzle

Contact Information: info@thewildrosepress.com

Cover Art by *Diana Carlile*

The Wild Rose Press, Inc.
PO Box 708
Adams Basin, NY 14410-0708

Visit us at www.thewilderroses.com

Publishing History
First Scarlet Rose Edition, 2015
Print ISBN 978-1-5092-0445-8
Digital ISBN 978-1-5092-0446-5

Published in the United States of America

He lives only for today…she has her eye on tomorrow.

"You know what I think, Victoria Templeton?" His soft voice sounded so very sexy as he moved to stand directly behind her, his nearness sending waves of heated desire coursing through her veins. "I think you've never done a spontaneous thing in your life."

"How dare you make such an assumption!" She whirled around to face him and found herself looking up into his mesmerizing blue eyes. She tried to force a confident tone into her voice, something she definitely didn't feel. "You don't know a thing about me or my situation."

"I'll even go so far as to guess that you don't know how to be spontaneous." He stared at her as if trying to reach inside her head and drag out her thoughts. "You're so busy worrying about tomorrow that you won't allow yourself any time for today."

"You think I don't know how to be spontaneous?" Her words were spoken half in anger and half in disbelief. He had challenged her, something she couldn't allow to go unanswered. She stepped close to him, wrapped her arms around his neck, and plastered her mouth against his.

PRAISE FOR AUTHOR

Samantha Gentry

AND HER BOOKS

FORBIDDEN ISLAND

"If you want a sexy read for a cool summer night, then I'd suggest Forbidden Island. I give this steamy short story 4.5 Cherries."

~Whipped Cream Reviews

STEAMY ENCOUNTER

"Samantha Gentry is an awesome writer who spins a tale of so much interest you have to fall in love with the characters and the book itself! Trust me on this! You will enjoy Ms. Gentry's style. I guarantee it...read this book!"

~5 Hearts - Brenda Tally, The Romance Studio

MASKED ENCOUNTER

"I found Masked Encounter a lovely and steamy way to spend a couple of hours. This is another story that will be placed prominently in my short story library."

~Joyfully Reviewed

UNEXPECTED ENCOUNTER

"Ms. Gentry has believable characters that are well written. She tells a visual tale with words."

~5 Angels - Dawnie, Fallen Angel Review

Chapter One

"Who…who are you?" Victoria Templeton froze in the open doorway, her key still in the front door lock. A quick surge of adrenaline jumped her heartbeat into high gear. "What are you doing in my house?"

A man in his late thirties, carrying a colorful box kite, stopped in mid-stride just inside the sliding glass door from the deck. He eyed her with curiosity, dropping his gaze to the floor then slowly letting it climb up her body until he made eye contact. His obvious scrutiny sent a nervous tremor darting across the surface of her skin.

"That should be my question. Who are you, and how did you get a key to *my* house?" His voice had a practiced smoothness, the kind that caused her nipples to pucker and her thoughts to wander. It didn't suggest anything threatening on his part, but it also did nothing to soothe the apprehension shoving at her.

"*Your* house?" She took a calming breath, but it didn't lessen the shiver caused by the way his intense blue eyes so blatantly looked her over—a shiver due as much to her immediate physical awareness of him as to the unsettling circumstances. She attempted to dismiss the tingle of attraction while trying, without much success, to hide her nervousness.

"I looked at this house two weeks ago, signed a rental agreement after lunch today, and now I'm moving in." Her precise, emphatic words failed to convey the control she hoped to project. "I don't know what you're doing here, but I insist you leave immediately, or I'll be forced to call the police."

"Whoa! Hold on." He placed the kite on the floor and closed the sliding door. "You're the one who's made a mistake. I have a signed one year lease, and I moved in over a week ago."

That one sentence wiped out the stranger's sexy persona. Vicki couldn't hide the shocked expression she knew must surely cover her face. "How can that be?" A hint of anxiety crept into her voice. "I was at the rental agent's office just a few hours ago. I paid the rental agreement in full and picked up the key. This was the only fully furnished house they had in this neighborhood available from May through September."

"Well, I suggest you go back to the agency, because this house is not available. I leased it from Gary Sanderson who owns this property and also happens to be a long-time friend of mine."

Her uneasiness gave way to indignant anger. "We'll see about that." She brushed a loose tendril of chestnut colored hair from her face. "I'm calling the agency right now."

He stepped aside, flashing a dazzling smile and causing her already puckered nipples to ache with need. A gush of moisture dampened her panties—both reactions involuntary and totally inappropriate for the situation.

"Be my guest. Feel free to use my phone if you'd like." He gestured toward the phone, then turned and walked away.

Vicki emitted a little sigh of relief after he retreated

to the kitchen, a response confirming just how disconcerting she found his presence. She forced her attention back to the problem at hand. Searching through her purse, she found the business card from the rental agency, picked up the handset of his phone from the charger, and dialed the number.

"Mr. Edwards, please. Victoria Templeton calling." She replaced the card in her purse, then glanced across the room. To her dismay, she spotted the stranger leaning against the kitchen doorjamb holding a bottle of beer. The way he seemed to be studying her caused a strange combination of nervous tremor and sexual need to sweep over her. She could not deny the primal desire coursing through her veins. *Primal desire? That's a laugh. I'm horny as hell, and he's drop dead sexy gorgeous.*

Dressed in cut-off jeans, a tank top, and no shoes, he stood maybe six-foot-one. Even though it was only the first week of May, his long legs, muscular arms, and broad shoulders displayed a nice tan. His dark blond hair contained lighter sun-bleached streaks although, in her opinion, a little too long and far too shaggy. Yet somehow very enticing. He looked more like an over-aged surfer than anything else, a man trying to retain his youth rather than concentrating on the important things in life—things such as working hard to provide a comfortable and secure future.

Her huff of indignation confirmed how he grated on her sense of the order of things. He didn't display the proper and prudent actions of someone striving for success. Regardless of how gorgeous he looked and that aura of pure sex surrounding him, he was obviously nothing more than a local beach bum who had somehow managed to gain access to her house. She shot him one last contemptuous look. Another little huff of disgust escaped her lips, signaling her opinion of his obvious lack of mature responsibility.

Still, something about him…a sort of animal magnetism that reached out and grabbed at the very core of her existence. Her pulse rate increased. A sensual surge raced through her body, sending another rush of moisture to the crotch of her panties.

She quickly dismissed the totally inappropriate, conflicting, and troubling thoughts, along with the unwelcome feelings that tried to gain a foothold in her normally sensible and well-ordered life. The last thing she needed—a physical attraction to this unacceptable man no matter how handsome, sexy, and desirable she found him. Regardless of the sensual impact he had on her body.

She returned her attention to her phone conversation as the other person came on the line.

"I'm sorry, Miss Templeton. Mr. Edwards has already left the office."

"What? That can't be. Is he gone for the weekend?" She glanced at her watch. Only four-thirty, a little early for a rental agent to disappear for the weekend in a beach community with summer approaching. "Is there someone else who can help me? There's a man here who claims to have signed a lease with the owner of this property, and he's already moved into *my* house. This is a totally unacceptable situation. I discussed my needs with Mr. Edwards in great detail. This is the only property that met all of my requirements."

"I'm only the answering service, not an agency

employee. All I can do is take a message."

Her words were not what Vicki wanted to hear. She glanced at the stranger again, who continued to lean against the doorjamb staring at her.

Blake Callahan took another swallow of his beer and studied the woman who had suddenly invaded his space. She definitely presented an unwanted interruption in his day. Not that he had anything special planned. In his life, one day had become like another. He shook his head, resigning himself to the fact she wasn't going to go away on her own. He would be forced to deal with the problem. He scrutinized her more closely.

She stood about five-foot-six, appeared to be approximately thirty years old, maybe a year or two more, and she wore her long hair pulled back at her nape fastened with a gold clasp. Her face showed a minimal amount of makeup. He studied her delicately sculpted features and bright hazel eyes, allowing that she would be truly beautiful if she replaced that scowl with a smile.

His gaze once again took in the entire woman. She wore a simple green T-shirt, its soft fabric caressing her full breasts and revealing the distinct outline of taut nipples. Her matching shorts showed off her shapely legs. He could almost feel them wrapped around his waist as her breasts pressed against him.

A tight sensation pulled across his chest and continued down to his groin. He took a deep breath in an attempt to break the constriction, but it didn't help—his response to her physical presence more akin to that of someone who hadn't had his cock inside a hot pussy in months rather than the reality of having enjoyed that pleasure only two days ago.

Nothing could be worth the concentrated amount of energy she seemed to be devoting to this. Life was much too short to be wasted on silly inconsequential mix-ups. For the past two years, he had embraced one philosophy above all others. Life needed to be lived for today because no one was guaranteed a tomorrow.

A little twinge of despair jabbed at his insides. The twinges had almost disappeared, but every now and then an errant one resurfaced as a cruel reminder of the past. He quickly buried the painful memory and raked his gaze across the contours of her breasts before lowering it to her crotch. She definitely wasn't wearing a bra. Did that lack of underwear extend to a lack of panties under those shorts? His cock twitched to life and threatened to stand at attention if he didn't divert his thoughts in a hurry. Her expression had turned from anger to distress. He concentrated on listening to her phone conversation as he stared out the window at the ocean.

"You're sure there's no one in the office who can settle this problem?" Her voice suddenly sounded less sure, more tentative. "Well, then...will you please contact Mr. Edwards and have him call me? I paid in advance for the entire five months with a cashier's check. I have a signed rental agreement..." Her words trailed off as if she didn't know what else to say.

The same determination she had displayed earlier—what he would call *aggressively pushy,* if he needed to label it—abruptly returned.

"This matter *must* be resolved today. I want this man out of my house immediately."

She listened to the person's response and replied in

a disappointed tone. "All right. I'll wait here until I hear from Mr. Edwards. The number is…" She stared at the phone for a second, then jerked her head up and looked at him.

She suddenly seemed to him more like a lost child trying to find her way in a confusing world rather than the uninvited intrusion who had invaded his day. Her helpless expression somehow managed to pierce his jaded exterior and struck a chord of sympathy and concern somewhere deep inside him, a place he hadn't realized still existed. No reason why he shouldn't let her wait for her phone call. She had already ruined what remained of his day. No purpose would be served by sending her away right now.

"I'm surprised you don't have a cell phone. I thought everybody had one." He gave her the number, then listened as she repeated it into the phone.

"And please, have someone get back to me as soon as possible." She gave him a nervous, almost apologetic sideways glance as she disconnected the call. "I know I should have one. My friends are amazed that I've been able to function without one. I've been meaning to get—"

"Hey, lady, how long am I supposed to hang around out here?" An angry male voice boomed into the room. "If you don't collect your stuff and pay me right now, I'm going to charge you a standby fee." The cab driver stood in the open front door, the expression on his face saying just as much as his angry words and tone of voice.

"I…" After another quick glance in Blake's direction, she returned her attention to the cab driver. Clenching her jaw in determination and squaring her shoulders, she gave the appearance of someone ready for a fight. "Bring my belongings into the house."

She reached for her purse and withdrew the money for the fare. It took the driver several trips to bring in her suitcases, plus six large cardboard cartons and a pet carrier containing a very upset Siamese cat.

The cab driver glared at Blake, obviously pissed because he didn't offer to help, then turned his frustration on Vicki. "Next time, lady, hire a moving van instead of a taxi."

The cabbie took the money she extended, his manner anything but gracious in spite of the generous tip she gave him. He slammed the minivan's door and sped away.

"Well...Victoria Templeton. I believe that's the name you gave on the phone." Blake had tried to appear calm as he watched the boxes and suitcases being stacked inside the front door, acutely aware of the emotion still jabbing at that vulnerable spot deep inside. The desire to jump her bones came as natural to him as breathing, but the emotional thread tugging at him presented a surprising and unacceptable situation. He hadn't been sure exactly what to do, so did nothing as the cab driver brought in her belongings.

He cast a wary eye toward the huge pile. A frown tugged at his forehead as his gaze landed on the caged animal making the type of loud, yowling noise only a Siamese cat could produce. "Does that animal always make such a racket?"

Her entire manner turned defensive. "Wouldn't you be unhappy if you were locked in a cage?" She quickly opened the pet carrier and removed the cat, gently stroking its fur as she talked to it. "Now, now.

Everything's okay. Is that better, Ty-Ling?"

When the cat calmed down, she placed it on the floor. It immediately darted out of sight behind the couch.

He scowled and glanced in the direction the cat had gone. Returning his attention to Vicki, his expression eased, and he crossed the room to where she stood. "Since you've taken it upon yourself to be my uninvited guest for a *short* while, I suppose I should introduce myself. I'm Blake Callahan." He held out his hand and offered her a polite, albeit uneasy, smile.

Vicki accepted his handshake. His smooth, un-callused skin confirmed her original opinion. He obviously didn't do any type of manual work, and his longish, shaggy hair ruled out the possibility of him being a business executive. She quickly withdrew her hand from his grasp as the rush of excitement caused her tummy to clench. His touch had been just a little too warm and intimate, and he seemed to hold her hand just a little bit longer than necessary. Or had she only imagined it?

He started toward the kitchen with his empty beer bottle, then turned back toward her. "Would you like something to drink? I have beer, wine, iced tea, water...or I could make some coffee."

"I, uh, yes, iced tea would be nice." She offered him a bit of a shy smile, not at all sure how to handle her inner conflict. "Thank you."

A twinge of nervousness darted through her as she noted the way he seemed to study her again. His alert blue eyes showed a surprising amount of intelligence, something obviously wasted by his lifestyle. His tanned good looks lingered on her senses, sending another totally inappropriate sensual tremor of desire racing through her body and settling deep inside her.

"Iced tea, it is. And when I return, I'd like to see a copy of your rental agreement." He turned and disappeared into the kitchen.

She called after him, "You want to see *my* rental agreement? Well, I insist on seeing *your* lease."

Who the hell did he think he was, challenging her veracity that way? Then another thought struck her. Why would he have opened the subject of leases if he didn't have one? Apprehension stirred deep inside her, leaving her unsettled. Maybe things weren't as clear cut as she had originally assumed...or as she wanted them to be.

Vicki looked around the living room of the house she thought she'd rented for the entire summer. The monthly rent had been a little more than she had planned to pay, but she fell in love with the house the moment the rental agent had shown it to her. A little frown wrinkled her forehead as she recalled the way Mr. Edwards had looked her over while making no effort to hide his lecherous intentions, not really all that different from the way Blake looked at her. But unlike Blake's scrutiny, the rental agent left her uncomfortable and feeling as if she needed a shower to wash away his visual groping.

The first floor of the two-story beach bungalow contained a comfortable living room with a wood burning fireplace and a separate dining room she had intended to use as her office. The living room opened onto a wraparound deck with a half dozen steps that led down to the wide, sandy beach. The bright, airy kitchen contained an island with a breakfast bar, plus a breakfast nook in a sunny corner. Beyond the kitchen, a separate laundry room and a full bathroom with an outside door from the deck.

The upstairs consisted of two large bedrooms, each with a door opening out to a common balcony that ran along the entire ocean side of the house. The balcony also served as a partial roof over the lower deck. The second floor had one full bathroom with a jetted tub and separate shower. The house came fully furnished, including dishes and cookware. It suited her needs exactly.

Blake emerged from the kitchen carrying a glass of iced tea and a bottle of beer. A quick flash of movement grabbed her attention, but not in time to prevent the inevitable disaster.

"Damn! What the hell—" The sound of breaking glass immediately followed his cry of pain. "Get the fuck off of me!"

He shook his leg in an attempt to dislodge the furry bundle with its claws firmly dug into his bare ankle. The cat finally broke off its attack and scampered away.

"Ty-Ling! You naughty cat." Vicki's first impulse had been to laugh at the animal's antics. The same thing had happened to her numerous times. Then she saw the pained expression on Blake's face and quickly banished any hint of amusement. "I'm so sorry. I'm afraid Ty-Ling gets a little cranky when she's been locked up in the carrier. I...I'll put her in another room." Vicki rushed toward the cat, who deftly squeezed behind the couch out of her reach.

"Look, Victoria—"

"Please..." She glanced awkwardly at the floor, then back at him. "Call me Vicki." Her embarrassment over the incident sent a heated flush across her cheeks. Her gaze darted nervously around the room in an attempt to avoid the disapproval she knew would be in his eyes.

"Look, *Vicki*..." His annoyance covered his face and filled his voice. "I'm standing here in my bare feet surrounded by broken glass. Do you think you can leave that holy terror of a cat alone long enough to give me a hand?"

His words elicited an immediate reaction inside her. What had been a heated flush of embarrassment turned into an incendiary moment of true mortification as her forehead heated up to match her cheeks. Her gaze leaped between the broken glass, his bare feet, and the place where the cat had disappeared behind the couch.

"Oh, I'm so sorry." She hurried toward the kitchen. "I'll get something to clean up this mess."

"No!" He snapped out the angry retort, his words stopping her sudden flurry of activity. "Go out to the deck and get my beach sandals so I can put something on my feet and move without fear of slicing them open."

"Of course." She headed for the large sliding glass door that led outside. As soon as she opened it, the room filled with the sounds of waves breaking on the sand and seagulls calling out to one another. She spotted a box kite flying in the wind with its line tied to the deck railing. A large, colorful wind sock fluttered from a pole on the corner of the roof.

She closed her eyes and allowed the late afternoon sun to warm her face. A smile tugged at the corners of her mouth. The gentle breeze jangled the wind chimes.

She took a deep breath, inhaling the fresh sea air. She loved the feeling of serenity the ocean provided, the inner calm chasing away all the anxieties and uncertainties that usually lived inside her.

"Fuck!" Blake's painful cry jerked her attention from her contemplation and back to him. She quickly grabbed the sandals from the deck and carried them inside.

"Damn cat." He reached down and took hold of the Siamese, pulling it away from the same ankle where it again dug its claws into his flesh, this time leaving deep scratches and several smears of blood. He held the squirming animal in both hands at arm's length in front of him. "You're definitely going to have to keep this wild beast locked up for the *short* duration of your stay." He flinched as the angry cat scraped its back claws against his arm in an effort to get away, leaving ugly red welts and blood.

"Oh, no. Oh, I'm so sorry. Not everyone likes cats." Vicki rushed to take the angry animal from him, quickly exchanging it for the sandals. Her embarrassment kept her from looking at him

He wiggled his feet into the sandals while she put the yowling animal back into the pet carrier. "Stop complaining, Ty-Ling. It's your own fault. If you hadn't been such a naughty girl, you wouldn't have to go back into your cage." She immediately returned her attention to Blake who was checking the damage to his ankle and arm. "Here, let me see."

She took his forearm and lightly touched the numerous scratches. "I'm so sorry about this, uh, Blake." Once again, the physical contact sent tremors of desire coursing through her. Desires that refused to be shoved aside. Embarrassment momentarily overruled the edgy situation building between them, supplanting any thought of physical attraction. "It doesn't look too bad. The bleeding has stopped. Do you have some antiseptic? I think cleaning is all it needs."

She looked up into his face. The muscles in his arm tensed when she made eye contact. Her heartbeat increased, followed by a momentary loss of breath. She didn't even want to acknowledge the sudden tingling between her legs.

Warmth swirled through Blake's body and shoved at his cock, her touch far more than merely soft and inviting. Something very different from when he merely lusted after a hot piece of ass. This represented a reality as disturbing as Vicki's physical presence in his house. He had noticed it when they shook hands and again when she took hold of his arm.

He withdrew from her touch as tactfully as he could. Just watching her made his cock twitch. And with physical contact added into the mix, regardless of how fleeting and casual, his arousal hardened. The unusual circumstances of the moment left him unsure about what to do. If they were in one of the many bars in the village, if he had met her at a party or even picked her up on the beach, he would know how to proceed. But this… She had not shown up at his door looking for fun and games, a night of no-strings-attached hot sex with a stranger.

Uncertainty filled the depths of her hazel eyes. He usually had no trouble putting people into categories and placing them within the structure of surrounding influences. He did it every day at work. Well, he *used to* do it every day, back when he worked for a living. In the days before…

He shoved away the unwelcome painful memory before it could get a foothold in his consciousness.

Blake thought he had already neatly categorized her, but Victoria Templeton turned out to be a bit of a puzzle. One moment an uptight, indignant woman determined to be in charge and the next minute she seemed shy and uncertain. "Look…you take care of *that* mess your cat made." He indicated the broken glass and spilled tea and beer, softening his voice in response to her obvious distress. "And I'll take care of *this* mess your cat made." He balanced on one foot and extended his other leg to display his wounded ankle while holding up his scratched arm.

"I'm so sorry about this. I apologize for Ty-Ling. I don't know what got into her. She's usually very well behaved." Her voice dropped to a near whisper, clearly conveying the sincerity of her words. "I feel so terrible about this."

"It's no big deal, really." An impulse or maybe an emotional desire that came from that vulnerable place he tried so hard to ignore pushed him to place his fingertips beneath her chin and lift her face until he could see her eyes again. "Don't worry about it." Uncertainty covered her face and the wariness clouded her eyes. "Do you always take everything so seriously?"

"I…I don't know what you mean." Vicki felt it again, the increased heartbeat and the shortness of breath. This stranger, this totally inappropriate and unacceptable man, had a disconcerting impact on her senses—one that left her wanting to know much more about him and, at the same time, left her confused and wary.

Her carefully planned future did not include a beach bum regardless of how sexy or the way he made her pussy tingle and her juices flow. The man with an important place in her life would be a hard worker. A responsible person with goals similar to hers, not some kite-flying, over-aged surfer type with no ambition, whose only redeeming qualities were a hard body, a handsome face, a killer smile, magnetic sex-appeal, and a mesmerizing voice.

He held her gaze a moment longer before dropping his hand and stepping back. "You'll find paper towels in the kitchen. I have some antiseptic upstairs in the bathroom." He shot a wary glance at the caged cat before heading toward the stairs.

She breathed a sigh of relief once he withdrew his fingers from beneath her chin, even though the sensual warmth of his touch lingered. Another tremor darted through her body. She shook it away and bent to collect the larger pieces of glass before going to the kitchen in search of paper towels.

After cleaning up, Vicki glanced toward the stairway. Blake had disappeared upstairs without another word. Hoping to be finished before he returned, she opened one of her cardboard cartons and took out the litter box and a bag of kitty litter, the cat's food and water bowls, and a container of cat food. She could not leave Ty-Ling confined inside the cage. Surely, it would be okay to temporarily house her cat in the laundry room with the door closed.

"Well, what do you think, Ty-Ling?" She opened the carrier and stroked the cat's fur. "Do you think you can leave Blake alone if I let you out? I know you don't like being locked in your cage, but you can't go around attacking him every time he crosses your path. Do you think you can be a good girl?"

The cat closed its eyes and purred contentedly. She stroked it for a moment longer before shutting it inside the laundry room.

Vicki took a quick look at her watch and wrinkled her brow into a frown. It was after five-thirty, and no one from the rental office had bothered to return her call. Something had to be resolved about exactly who had to leave and who could stay in the house. A touch of pique pulled at her sense of order when she recalled Blake's audacity in demanding to see her rental agreement. Well, maybe *demanding* wasn't exactly the right word, but he had definitely made the request in a rather emphatic tone.

****

Blake quickly tended to his injuries, then started toward the stairs. He paused at the top with his hand on the banister as haunting memories from the past, stirred to the surface by Vicki's unexpected intrusion into his life, filled his mind.

Retracing his steps, he entered his bedroom and closed the door behind him. He stood motionless in front of his closet for several seconds, then carefully took a box from the top shelf. It had been three months since he'd last looked at the contents of the box. He thought about Vicki. About the place inside him her situation had somehow managed to touch. A place he had carefully closed off behind an emotionless wall in hopes of keeping the pain tucked away. A place where a little spark of life and emotion still fought to survive.

Opening the box, he reached a trembling hand

inside and withdrew a photograph. His gaze landed on the picture of the little boy waving from the swing. He picked up another photo, this one of himself with the same little boy flying a kite at the beach. Then he withdrew a piece of paper, and a knot of emotion lodged in his throat. He unfolded the crayon drawing of a brightly colored kite flying in the blue sky. The words below it printed in a childish scrawl.

I love you, Daddy.

Another twinge of despair stabbed at Blake's heart, but he quickly shoved it away. It had been two years since the painful loss of his six year old son. He had easily dealt with the situation of his wife deserting them when Bobby was only a year old. After all, the accidental pregnancy had been the only reason for their marriage, and she had not really wanted the baby.

But losing his son had been almost more than he could handle. Bobby had been run down by a speeding car right in front of his eyes, and at that moment, a gaping hole had been ripped in his heart. His plans for the future—for his son—had been cruelly snatched away, leaving him drifting aimlessly without purpose. On that day, he stopped living. His life became nothing more than a day-to-day existence.

He could not bring himself to look at the other items in the box. Perhaps he would later. He carefully refolded the drawing and placed it back inside along with the photographs, then set the container on the dresser. Taking a steadying breath, he headed back to the living room.

The sound of Vicki's voice brought him to a halt at the foot of the stairs.

"But I don't understand. This is the answering

service? How can there not be anyone available to help me until Monday? What happened to the person I was speaking with just a little while ago? I explained the situation to her. Someone was supposed to get back to me today. There's a man living in the house I rented, and he claims to have a lease. This situation must be cleared up immediately. All of my belongings are here. I don't have a car or any other means of moving my things again, and I have no place else to stay. I paid five months' rent in advance."

Desperation filled her voice, touching Blake in ways that shocked him. He went straight to the desk and returned with the copy of his lease. Then he watched and listened as she concluded her conversation.

She seemed so distraught and in need of help. Again, a little flicker of life tried to warm that cold place deep inside him where he had locked away his emotions. The words caught in his throat, but he finally managed to force them out. "Vicki, I—"

She jumped at the sound of his voice. "You startled me. I didn't hear you come downstairs."

"I'm sorry you're having so much trouble." He offered a sincere smile. "Obviously, the rental agency doesn't intend to deal with this screw-up until Monday. Gary Sanderson, the owner of the house, is out of town for the weekend. That's probably what the rental people discovered, so they ducked out without resolving their mistake, leaving you to fend for yourself."

She didn't utter a word, but her look of despair said it all.

"Did I hear you say you paid for May through September in advance with a cashier's check?" His words were a vague, half-formed thought that had somehow managed to escape into the open of its own volition.

Vicki nodded.

"That's odd. It doesn't sound like the type of thing Gary would do." He handed her the piece of paper in his hand. "This is a copy of my lease. As you can see from the date, I do have prior claim on this house."

She hesitantly reached for the offered document. She stared at the piece of paper, then heaved a sigh of resignation and sank onto the couch. The hopelessness of the situation reflected in her eyes when she returned the paper to him.

"I...I don't know what to do. I have my business to take care of. I planned to use the dining room as my office. I don't own a car. This house is conveniently located just a couple of blocks walk from the village and my clients." She looked around the room, sadness edging into her voice. "It was all so perfect."

"Business? What do you do?"

"I'm an accountant."

Blake managed to hide his surprise. She certainly didn't look like the stereotypical image of an accountant—not with that body, a very tempting mouth, and those eyes.

"I've contracted with several of the summer seasonal businesses in the village to have them as my clients. I need someplace large enough to let me work, and yet close enough so not having a car won't be a problem. I also need something fully furnished." She again looked around the living room. "This was the only house that fit all those needs. This is where my clients are, so this is where I need to be." Her voice faltered. "Now I don't know what I'm going to do."

"You're doing this just for the summer? What do you do the rest of the year? Where do you normally live and work?"

"Until a week ago, I worked for a large insurance company. I plan to return to the university in the fall. I've been saving my money so I can go straight through to get my master's degree while living on campus without having to hold down a job. That way, I can take a heavier class schedule and finish sooner."

Vicki firmly believed that would provide her with the means of guaranteeing a secure future without any reliance on anyone else—a sense of security all important to her carefully orchestrated life. "That's why I don't have a car. I sold it to pay the rent on this house. I decided it was a good trade off, since I can make more money over the summer here than if I continued for the next few months at my old job."

"Sounds like a pretty ambitious program."

"You can't just sit around and assume things will work out by themselves." Her indignation made its way into her voice despite her obvious attempts to keep it out. "It takes hard work and planning for the future."

"Really? Is your entire life already planned out, with every minute accounted for in your schedule? Do you have any time set aside to have fun? To enjoy what life has to offer?"

"I…" Vicki suddenly felt as if she were under a microscope, her entire life and philosophy being dissected, studied in detail, and challenged. She set her jaw in determination and brushed at an imaginary tendril of hair. "There will be plenty of time for *that* later. Right now, it's important for me to plan for a secure future."

She rose, crossed the room to the sliding glass door, and stared out at the ocean. The only thing in her life to occur on an unscheduled basis was hot sex when someone special stimulated her desires. She took a calming breath in an attempt to stop the unwanted throbbing in her pussy. Someone exactly like this man—the totally unacceptable, yet physically desirable Blake Callahan.

Anger welled inside her. How dare this stranger challenge and ridicule what she held as so important to her life? He obviously didn't know a thing about maintaining a proper sense of responsibility. She turned and glared at him.

"I don't know what you do for a living, assuming you actually *do* some type of work." She shot a pointed barb at him. "But I intend to make sure my future is properly secured. I have no intention of wasting my time on frivolous nonsense. Besides—"

Tears welled in her eyes. She quickly blinked them away, not sure if they were tears of anger, righteous indignation, or some deeper sense that something very important was missing from her life. "My mother never had a washer and dryer!"

Chapter Two

"Your mother never had a washer and dryer?" A look of total bewilderment covered Blake's face. "What the hell does that mean?" He tilted his head and stared at her, his eyebrows knitted in a confused frown. "I haven't the vaguest idea what you're talking about. Are you trying to save money so you can buy your mother a washer and dryer?"

"It's nothing." Vicki clipped her words as she spit out the thought. Her defenses were definitely up. "You obviously wouldn't understand."

Maybe others had time to waste their lives on frivolous pursuits like flying kites, but not her. As a child, her father had moved their family from city to city and state to state, always in search of the *big break* just over the hill in the next town. She had grown up in one small rented apartment after another. She needed the sense of security that had been lacking in her childhood, the permanency her mother never had. The washer and dryer had become symbols of the security and permanency she vowed to provide for herself.

She had worked hard to further her education and map out her future. Her bachelor's degree had been a slow process. From the time she graduated from high school, she had worked full time to support herself in addition to paying her college expenses. After that, she set her goal on the pursuit of a master's degree. Her goal was finally within sight. She would have time to indulge in *frivolous* things after she had firmly established her own business and secured her future.

Vicki had watched her mother haul loads of laundry for their family of five to the coin operated public laundry during all the years of her childhood and youth. And even though she never heard her mother complain, she surely must have resented the extra burden she shouldered to allow her father to follow his dreams without accepting the responsibilities a family required. Well, that would not be her lot in life. She had her feet firmly planted in reality.

She would have her washer and dryer.

"How do you know I wouldn't understand? Why don't you give me a try? You might be surprised."

"It's…it's not important. Forget it."

"Okay, if you'd rather not talk about it."

She stared out the window as her last remnant of control over the situation slipped away.

"Uh, I have a suggestion that could help you out of your predicament, at least for the moment. This is a large house. Perhaps we could reach an understanding about sharing it until Monday, when you can work out something with the rental office."

Her eyes widened as shock traveled through her body. Had she heard him correctly?

He awkwardly shifted his weight from one foot to the other, uncertainty showing on his face. "I know it sounds kind of bizarre, especially since we don't know anything about each other, but give it some thought. You don't need to be alarmed. I'm not the type to sneak up on you in the middle of the night while you're sleeping and jump into your bed." A teasing grin slowly spread across his face. "At least not without an invitation."

Wariness replaced her initial shock, and she took a couple of steps backward.

His expression turned serious. "Lighten up a little. I'm just kidding. There's no reason for you to be worried about your safety. So, what do you think? Can we co-exist for a couple of days?"

"Well…" It took her a few seconds to get over her alarm. She hesitated as she tried to formulate her thoughts and weigh her alternatives. Between the rental agency not calling her back and Blake showing her a copy of a signed lease, she had little doubt about the legitimacy of his claim to the house. She pulled open the sliding glass door to let in the sounds of the ocean and took a deep breath to calm her inner jitters. She tried to put her heated physical desire for this totally inappropriate man to one side so she could make a logical evaluation of the situation. "I can't make a decision like this without considering all the facets of the problem and carefully weighing the pros and cons."

"You know what I think, Victoria Templeton?" His soft voice sounded so very sexy as he moved to stand directly behind her, his nearness sending waves of heated desire coursing through her veins. "I think you've never done a spontaneous thing in your life."

"How dare you make such an assumption!" She whirled around to face him and found herself looking up into his mesmerizing blue eyes. She tried to force a confident tone into her voice, something she definitely didn't feel. "You don't know a thing about me or my situation."

"I'll even go so far as to guess that you don't know

how to be spontaneous." He stared at her as if trying to reach inside her head and drag out her thoughts. "You're so busy worrying about tomorrow that you won't allow yourself any time for today."

"You think I don't know how to be spontaneous?" Her words were spoken half in anger and half in disbelief. He had challenged her, something she couldn't allow to go unanswered. She stepped close to him, wrapped her arms around his neck, and plastered her mouth against his. Her breasts pressed against his hard chest. Then, very aware of his rapidly growing erection, she leaned her hips against his body.

Oh, God...he feels so good.

She could imagine that impressive cock sliding inside her. Her pussy tingled with need. It had been too long since she enjoyed a wild, raunchy tumble in the sack. Her vibrator continued to be a dependable friend in a time of need but didn't provide an adequate replacement for the real thing. Damn, what was it about this totally unsuitable man that had her wanting to rip off the few clothes he was wearing, shove him down on the floor, and impale herself on his stiff cock?

His tongue probed between her lips. She opened her mouth, allowing the texture of his tongue to mesh with hers. The sensation of his hand sliding down her back and across her hip to cup her ass sent a shiver of anticipation racing through her body.

Blake pulled her tighter against him. It had taken him a moment to get over his shock at her suddenly aggressive manner. One thing was for sure—no way could this woman *ever* be classified cold as ice. Not if the earthiness of her kiss was any indication. It made him want to bury his cock deep inside her, and as soon as possible. His original plan for the night had been to wander into the village and grab one of the beach bunnies for yet another night of hot, meaningless sex, maybe even a threesome, but he would much prefer to explore the hidden talents of Vicki Templeton.

He ran his hand under her T-shirt and cupped the fullness of her bare breast. Her creamy smooth skin excited his senses.

Then, to his surprise, she broke off the kiss and took a step back. Her slightly parted, kiss-swollen lips begged for more, as did the raw passion burning in the depths of her eyes. His ragged breathing matched hers. He reached for her, but she deftly moved out of his immediate range. Was she playing some kind of teasing game? If so, he would have her out the door and on her way pronto. He didn't have any trouble taking no for an answer and letting his pursuit of a woman drop. But he had no use for cock teasers and no interest in women who wanted to play little games of temptation while knowing they had no intention of following through. Fantasy games with whipped cream, body paint, and sex toys were an entirely different situation.

"I guess that proves I'm capable of being spontaneous."

"So that's what this is about?" He studied the determination covering her face, a look that did not match the passion still smoldering in her eyes. "Your need to *prove* something?"

She stared at him in disbelief.

"And did you manage to prove whatever it was?" He tried, but he couldn't keep the sarcasm out of his voice.

She squared her shoulders while tugging at the

bottom of her T-shirt to smooth it down. "Yes, I believe so. I proved I can be spontaneous if I choose to. I also put the, uh, *tension* to rest so we can resolve the real problem without veering off course." She paused as if to collect her thoughts. Her inner conflict showed on her face as her manner softened. "Look, I don't mean to sound unappreciative of your offer. It's just that, well, these are unusual circumstances, and I don't know a thing about you. For instance, what do you do for a living?"

Put the tension to rest? Those may have been her words, but they hadn't come anywhere near to doing that, as far as he could tell. Not only did the sexual tension continue to exist, it had doubled. His mind reeled from her abrupt change of direction. She had gone from hot passion to cool logic in a matter of seconds.

Now his turn had come to decide what kind of personal information to reveal, and what to keep safely hidden away. He carefully chose his words. "I'm...I guess you could say I'm retired."

Her expression went blank as she stared at him, as if she hadn't heard what he said. Then she apparently found her voice. "You're *retired?* You aren't old enough. What you mean is that you're unemployed." Her abject disapproval came through loud and clear.

He had earned a Doctorate of Sociology, and at his current age of thirty-nine was the youngest department head at the university. In fact, the youngest in the university's history. Following his son's death, he had tried to bury himself in academic duties but found each term more difficult to endure than the one before. So just prior to the beginning of the spring term, he had made the decision to take a one year sabbatical.

He sold his house near the university, had sold everything but his clothes, car, and a few other personal items, and signed the one year lease on the beach house that belonged to his friend, Gary Sanderson.

The work ethic that had driven him to his early success no longer held any importance. He found it necessary to live each day as it came, to throw off the yoke of his previous life, and to make decisions predicated on what he wanted at the moment rather than on what was deemed proper, acceptable, or practical. Building toward a future no longer mattered. No one was guaranteed a tomorrow. Not even this compulsively regimented woman who had suddenly invaded his life.

"Look, Vicki. It's dinner time, and I'm hungry." Blake's exasperation resounded in his voice. "Do you want me to help take your suitcases upstairs to the spare room, or do you need to use the phone to make a motel reservation and call a taxi? Hopefully, you won't get the same driver who brought you here."

"I, well..." She nervously cleared her throat. "All right, I'll accept your offer. But I must warn you. I know karate and...and I have a gun."

He couldn't stop the open, easy laugh that shattered the tension filling the room. "Well, I don't know karate, and I don't own a gun." He tilted his head to one side and studied her for a moment, a teasing grin playing across his lips. "And judging by your flamboyant display of spontaneity, maybe I'm the one who'd better make sure my bedroom door is locked."

"I—I didn't mean to insinuate that—" She turned her back to him, but not quickly enough to prevent him from seeing her face and neck turn crimson with embarrassment.

"The second bedroom at the end of the hall is yours." Blake didn't say anything else. He simply grabbed her suitcases and took them upstairs. When he came back down, he went straight out onto the deck.

He had a kite to reel in. He untied the line from the railing and brought the colorful box kite down, setting it inside the living room next to the one he'd placed there earlier. Standing on the deck, he looked at the panorama spread out before him. It had been a beautiful, sunny day with only a few clouds on the horizon. The sunset promised to be a dazzling one, the type to be savored and enjoyed rather than merely accepted as the norm.

"Yo, Blake!" The shout came from down the beach.

Blake raised his hand to shade his eyes from the sunlight. He spotted his next door neighbor walking across the sand toward him. "Hey, Tim. What's up?"

Blake had met his gregarious, fun-loving neighbor the first day he moved into the beach house. Tim Flannigan was a partner in a very successful law firm but only went into the city two or three days a week. He could accurately be described as a playboy who lived life in the fast lane.

Tim stopped next to the deck railing where Blake stood. "Party at my place on Saturday, a week from tomorrow, starting at seven o'clock and lasting until…oh, maybe the entire weekend." He flashed his practiced smile, his dark eyes twinkling with good fun. "It's going to be a night of wine, women, and song, and you can forget about the song part."

"Sounds good." Blake's good-natured laugh fit in with Tim's fun-loving mood. "What's the occasion?"

"The summer season's almost upon us, meaning beach bunnies in thongs with bouncing boobs. Tits and ass everywhere." He waved his arm across the expanse of the sand, indicating the entire scene. "As far as the eye can see. All the pussy you can handle." Tim turned and headed back to his house.

Blake called out after him. "Are we still on for volleyball tomorrow?"

"You bet." Tim waved as he climbed the steps to his own deck. "See you at ten."

Blake took a deep breath and filled his lungs with clean ocean air. He thought about Tim's party and the type of people who would probably be there. It was impossible to ignore the continual parade of women coming and going from Tim's house. For the most part, it looked to him as if Tim had no interest in intellectual stimulation and had an incredible interest in vacuous beach bunnies with artificially enhanced attributes.

Then he thought of the parade of women who'd been in and out of his *own* life the last couple of years. He had to admit he couldn't find much difference between them even though he tried to rationalize his own behavior and definitely needed the occasional intelligent conversation to break the mindless whirl.

When his son died, he had lost all interest in trying to find the one woman who would make them a true family. Instead, he settled for a life of parties, mindless pleasure fucking, and living only for the day without the troublesome interference of things like emotions.

Then there was the night he'd spent with the identical twins. Even their body piercings were identical. One ring in the left nipple and a ring through the outer right pussy lip. The only way to tell them apart was by the tattoo on their inner thighs—a rose for one twin and a butterfly for the other. His first *ménage a trois*. On a physical level, it had been exciting. But on a deeper level, it had turned out to be as empty as the rest of his life had become.

He leaned against the railing and watched the sky change from blue to pink and gold as the sun dipped closer and closer to the horizon.

"I'm settled into my room."

Vicki's voice surprised him. He had been so absorbed in his own world he hadn't heard her walk out onto the deck. He glanced toward her. "Good."

Vicki took a calming breath, but it didn't help much. Awkwardness suddenly permeated the air, discomfort resulting from the fact that, for all intents and purposes, they were now officially living together…if only for the weekend. Two strangers with absolutely nothing in common other than one hot kiss.

The uncomfortable sensation tightened across her chest, as if everything had suddenly started to close in around her and she had no control over any of it. Taking Blake up on his offer had been the only logical thing to do. Even if she could conduct her business from a motel room, which she knew she would not be able to do, she certainly could not afford to stay in a motel for very long. If only she hadn't paid Mr. Edwards for the entire five months in advance. But the *if only* didn't matter. She had paid the money and had to face the current situation as it stood, rather than the way she wanted it to be.

The memory of Blake's delicious kiss continued to

tingle through her all the way to her toes. Her entire body vibrated with pent up sexual desire. No way could she lie to herself and pretend she didn't want him in every way possible. But for now, clearer heads needed to prevail. She needed to make the best of the obviously awkward situation.

He gestured toward the ocean. "We have the beginnings of a beautiful sunset."

"Shouldn't we be preparing dinner?"

He stared at her for a moment. "You consider relaxing and taking in the beauty of a sunset a waste of time?"

"It doesn't seem a very constructive use of time when other things need to be done." The disapproval of his stare burned into her, but it only reinforced her opinion that she was right.

"You know..." He reached out and touched her cheek with his fingertips, sending a tremor of desire through her body. "You'll be so busy working for tomorrow, that one day you'll wake up and realize your only memories are of empty yesterdays."

She held his gaze for a long moment. Turmoil and confusion filled her consciousness. What he'd said was completely wrong and in direct opposition to everything she held dear. So why was her stomach doing flip-flops?

She brushed away the imaginary tendril of hair and tried to assert herself. "You're wrong. You shouldn't waste time drifting through life without purpose, as if tomorrow will never come. Perhaps that philosophy works for you now, but one day you'll be the one who wakes up and finds he has nothing in life."

"There's no guarantee you'll have a tomorrow." He

turned back toward the horizon.

She didn't understand the sadness and despair that filled his voice, but it tugged hard at her emotions. In an attempt to avoid the unexpected upheaval bubbling inside her, she turned the conversation to what she hoped would be a safer topic.

"Well, I guess the next order of business is dinner." She forced an upbeat attitude, one she didn't feel. "Let me prepare the meal. It's the least I can do to repay you for your generosity. I'll keep an accurate listing of my portion of the expenses and reimburse you fully. I don't want you to be inconvenienced by this temporary situation…at least not any more than you already have been."

What she found in his refrigerator and cupboards came as a pleasant surprise—fresh fruits and vegetables, along with chicken and fish, a nice selection of herbs and spices for cooking. Apparently his kitchen skills were a lot more advanced than just popping something frozen into the microwave. She also noted several bottles of good quality wine. He may be nothing more than a kite-flying, unemployed beach bum, but somewhere along the line he had cultivated a taste for gracious living.

A tight puckering of her nipples accompanied her increased heartbeat. He had intensified her existing itch of need. Did she dare contemplate letting him relieve that itch?

She immediately berated herself for indulging in totally improper thoughts about a weekend of wild, uninhibited sex with someone she'd just met—someone she deemed totally unacceptable. She had her work, her plans, and her goals for the future. She did not have time for some shiftless stranger, no matter how sexy or how much he made her pulse race and her pussy throb.

She turned her attention to fixing dinner. And along with that came a curious thought. *Retired? That's a joke. How can an unemployed kite-flying beach bum afford to live in my house?* A huff of disgust left her throat. Signed lease be damned. He was probably mooching off his friend who owned the house.

****

Blake turned over and pounded his pillow into a more comfortable shape. The clock in the living room chimed one o'clock. Other than that, the house remained quiet, with the only sound coming from the waves breaking on the beach.

He had been asleep when some sort of noise awakened him. He listened for it but didn't hear anything else. Unfortunately, he was now wide awake and unable to get back to sleep. Maybe having something to eat would help. He pulled on a pair of sweat pants and went downstairs. After rummaging around in the refrigerator, he found a piece of cold chicken left over from dinner.

It had been a tasty meal. Vicki had proven to be a good cook. He nibbled on the chicken as he walked into the living room, finally coming to a halt in front of the doors leading to the deck. The moonlight shimmered across the water, giving an eerie glow to the waves as they broke against the sand. His thoughts darted between his lost son, the emptiness of his life, and the bleakness of his future. Then he focused on the disturbing presence of the compulsively ordered woman asleep in his spare bedroom. A woman who stirred much more in him than he wanted to admit, both physically and emotionally.

"What the—" He jumped aside as soft fur brushed across the top of his bare foot, then wrapped around his ankle. Well, at least the four-legged beast refrained from digging its claws into him this time. He bent down and caught the animal before it could scamper out of reach.

"Tell me, cat…what's the story with your owner?" He stroked Ty-Ling's fur and continued to stare out the door. The cat squirmed in his arms in an effort to get loose but didn't scratch him. "I've never seen anyone so obsessed with planning for the future. And that bit about the washer and dryer… It's all very strange. Then she planted a kiss on me that nearly had my cock standing up straight and begging for more."

The light in the living room snapped on, startling him with the sudden intrusion. He whirled around and squinted against the brightness. Vicki stood across the room, her hand on the light switch. The soft waves of her chestnut hair hung down almost to her shoulders. Her peach-colored silk robe reached halfway down her thighs, well above her knees.

"Oh, I didn't realize you were down here. I wanted a drink of water." Vicki noticed Ty-Ling squirming as Blake put the cat on the floor. She rushed toward him to take possession of the animal before it had a chance to attack. "I'm so sorry she annoyed you again. I told her to quit attacking you. I guess she didn't listen. If—if she's bothering you, I can shut her back in the laundry room."

"It's okay. The furry little terror didn't dig its claws into me this time. We were just getting acquainted."

Her eyes gravitated to Blake's physique—his broad shoulders, the wisps of sandy-colored hair scattered across his hard chest, his flat belly, the way his sweat pants rested low on his hips, and the obvious bulge at his crotch that said he wasn't wearing anything under his sweat pants. Did he sleep in the nude? She tightened the sash at the waist of her robe, acutely aware of the way the soft silk caressed her bare breasts, causing her nipples to pucker. She forced down the sudden nervousness that welled inside her. A moment of eye contact said he wanted her as much as she wanted him. Moisture seeped from between her pussy lips, dampening the curls adorning her mound.

He grasped her hand and pulled her toward him. "You have every right to say no." His words came out in a husky whisper. "And I'll respect your decision."

He paused for what seemed to her like an eternity but in reality only a few seconds, before tugging at her sash until it came undone and the front of her robe fell open. The sparkle in his eyes followed his quick intake of breath as he raked his gaze over her nude body. Her insides quivered with excitement when he traced his fingertip across the curves of her breasts. Bending forward, he took one of her taut nipples into his mouth, held it there for a second, and then released it.

"If you don't say something right now, I'm going to take you to my bed and spend the rest of the night fucking you until you're totally satisfied in every way and neither of us has the strength to move. Then I'm going to start all over again."

She stroked his erection through the fabric of his sweat pants, knowing her action would speak louder than words. She had made her decision the moment he said he intended to spend the night satisfying her. Blake Callahan represented much more than a very sexy man. He would also be a generous lover. And if the feel of his hard cock and the way it made her pussy gush provided any indication, he would be an exciting lover, too.

Her brief marriage had been a disaster, and that included a totally lackluster sex life, which probably explained her strong sex drive now. Her ex-husband had only been concerned with his own satisfaction, as if she didn't have needs. He didn't seem to care if she had an orgasm or not as long as he did. It never varied. He'd climb on, shove his cock in and out of her a few times, and come. When he finished, he'd roll off, tweak her nipple while telling her how great it had been, then fall asleep.

She spent many nights fighting frustration while trying to get to sleep. And many days with her vibrator while he was at work. That frustration led to the occasional thought of having an affair, but she had always rejected the idea. Adultery and infidelity were not acceptable to her. As long as she was married, she would be true to her vows.

The sexual frustration coursing through her body told her how much she wanted to sample Blake Callahan's prowess, to have his cock buried deep inside her as they explored the many facets of hot sex and heated passion.

He took her hand and headed for the stairs, flipping off the light as they started toward the second floor. Once inside his bedroom, she discarded her robe and he dropped his sweat pants to the floor. The thought that she had only known this man for a few hours—and spent most of that time locked in confrontation with him—briefly crossed her mind. She also allowed the thought that since they temporarily resided in the same house, neither of them had the availability of going home afterward. Whatever the results of their lovemaking, whether awkward or satisfying, they would be together through the entire weekend.

But one look at Blake's magnificent cock standing at attention swept all speculation and concerns from her mind. The memory of their passionate kiss told her everything she needed to know. She wanted that cock. Losing herself in his passion was the only thing that mattered at that moment. Logic tried to push its way in with practical thoughts that should have prevailed over physical desire. But she managed to ignore them.

He may have been far removed from the proper, hard-working professional type of man with whom she would choose to spend her future, but he represented everything she needed at the moment. Was that selfish of her? Did it make her a jaded, wanton woman without redeeming qualities? Did it make her superficial without any depth?

Then he cupped her bare breast and claimed her mouth with his, and her thoughts stopped.

Chapter Three

Blake captured Vicki's mouth with a hot kiss, making a promise of ecstasy yet to come. His tongue darted into the dark recesses of her mouth, exploring and tasting. Her tongue twined with his in a mating ritual of sorts, their textures meshing in sensual togetherness. His hard cock pressed against her belly, causing her entire body to tremble with anticipation and expectation.

She reached for his erection and grazed her fingertips along the underside of his rigid shaft. The tantalizing sensation, in addition to its extreme hardness, left her fingers tingling. Her pussy throbbed with an intense desire to have him inside her. She wanted—*needed*—to explode in orgasm.

He broke off the kiss, but only long enough to snuggle her body into the softness of his king-sized bed and situate himself between her spread legs with his stomach pressing against her wet center. Her full breasts stood firm, capped by dusky pink nipples. He teased one with the tip of his tongue, then the other before drawing it into his mouth. He sucked each nipple in turn. Her soft moans of delight became groans of need as her increased arousal expanded her desires. Passionate kisses became hungry kisses as he licked and nibbled his way down her body.

Vicki's core muscles contracted sharply when his

hot breath grazed the sensitive skin of her inner thighs. She reached down and tangled her fingers in his thick hair but didn't need to use pressure to guide his head or to shove her pussy against his mouth in an attempt to feed her own needs. Every flick of his tongue, every place his lips touched, sent tremors of excitement coursing through her body. His tongue parted her pussy lips, darting in and out with light, delicate strokes one moment, and teasing her engorged clit the next. Her chest heaved with her labored breathing. She kneaded her breasts and plucked at her nipples as his stimulation increased. Her entire body trembled with rapidly growing excitement. His very talented mouth had her teetering on the edge of rapture.

Then he caught her clit with his lips, sucked it into his mouth, and inserted two fingers into her wet channel. She cried out and jerked her hips off the bed. Waves of ecstasy crashed through her body. Convulsions started deep inside her and quickly spread. But he didn't let up. He continued to devour her clit while stroking his fingers in and out of her opening. Then his ardor increased, and his mouth became even more insistent. She spiraled into an unending orgasm unlike anything she had ever experienced.

It wasn't always easy for her to reach orgasm. A man with only marginal skills...well, he might be entertaining, but that wasn't the same thing as satisfying. But Blake Callahan's attentions to her pussy at that moment... She couldn't even wrap her mind around the enormity of the incredible sensations. Her inner walls continued to clench in tight contractions, grabbing and tugging at his fingers. Her clit felt as if it would explode. She thrashed her head back and forth on the pillow, shut her eyes tightly, and opened her mouth. Was it possible to die from orgasmic rapture? Could a person literally overdose on phenomenal sex? If so, then what a way to go.

Blake finally lifted his head. His gaze landed on her, on the flush of orgasm tinting her face with a sensual glow, and his chest heaved. He licked his lips and continued to stroke his fingers in and out of her wet opening, but at a slower pace.

Her erratic movements finally tapered off, and her eyelids fluttered open. Passion blazed in the depths of her eyes. The tip of her tongue darted sensually back and forth as she licked her lips. Her hair framed her face in wild disarray. He had never seen anyone more desirable, with a look of sensual, earthy abandon, or more naturally beautiful than she was at that moment.

The sight of her pulled at his emotions in the same manner she had from the moment he'd first encountered her. Something about her truly reached out and grabbed him. This was more than just another mindless, hot fuck. He didn't know why. He wished it wasn't so, but he didn't know how to stop it. What he did know was that he wanted more of her, and he wanted it now.

Vicki scooted into a sitting position, then rose onto her knees. She applied a slight pressure on his shoulder, indicating what she wanted him to do. He rolled over onto his back. His rock-hard cock bobbed in the air, its long, thick shaft capped with a dark purple head. She leaned forward, wrapped her hand around its girth, and lapped at the head with the flat of her tongue.

He groaned as she opened her mouth and closed her lips around his shaft. A groan from deep inside him, one of intense pleasure, clawed its way out of his throat.

A tight sensation spread across his chest, grabbing at his nerve endings each time her lips slid down to take more of his length into her mouth. Her lips maintained a tight seal, creating a delicious friction that excited his senses. Her mouth performed magic, sending his euphoria soaring to new heights. This couldn't possibly be the same woman who seemed obsessed with working for the future while today took a back seat. Yet it was.

He moved her over to grab a condom from the nightstand drawer, and she allowed his cock to slide from her mouth.

Vicki couldn't explain her need for Blake Callahan. Maybe it was something about their body chemistry, something in the air, or something in the food they had for dinner. Perhaps even something in the water supply. She didn't know what caused it. All she knew was that she couldn't get enough of him. Right or wrong didn't matter. Should or shouldn't had become totally irrelevant. He was not the type of man who fit into her neatly organized, planned out life. Not the right man at all.

But at the moment, it didn't matter.

She placed a kiss on his cock head, then ran the tip of her tongue along the underside of his shaft. Grinning seductively, she took the packet from his hand and ripped it open. "Do you want to roll this on or should I do it for you?"

"Well, given the option, I'd prefer for you to do the deed."

They made eye contact, a moment that became frozen in time as they continued to hold each other's gaze. A sense that something very special was about to happen filled the air around them. It lasted only a few seconds, but left an irreversible impression.

Vicki rolled the condom onto Blake's stiff erection. Her pussy still tingled from the intensity of the multiple orgasms he had given her with his mouth. She throbbed with the need to feel him buried deep inside her. How could she still be experiencing need rather than want? A simple answer—more was happening here than merely the two of them satisfying a physical need. She *wanted* Blake Callahan, as totally illogical and inappropriate as that sounded. She wanted him in any and every way possible. And she definitely needed him to fulfill the desire he had created.

He pulled her down onto the bed next to him and gently sucked each of her breasts, then moved upward to capture her mouth in a kiss filled with much more than naked lust. Wrapping his arms around her, he held her close. They rolled over, with Vicki on her back and him on top. Without breaking the kiss, he slowly entered her, inch-by-inch, until his cock became fully embedded inside her, stretching her in a most pleasurable way.

She wrapped her legs around his hips as he delved inside her, matching each of his down strokes with an upward thrust of her hips until they established a smooth rhythm and moved in complete harmony. She teetered so close to the edge from her previous orgasm, it took him only a few strokes to envelope her in continuing waves of orgasmic bliss. She gasped for air, her lungs not able to take in oxygen fast enough. His marvelous cock completely filled her, reaching to the depths of her tunnel. No man had ever driven her to the heights of ecstasy that he did.

But she didn't have a place in her life for a shiftless beach bum. She had everything planned out, and that plan couldn't be changed. Besides, a relationship between them would never work. He was not what she envisioned—the stable, organized, hard-working type of man who would fit in with her plan for the future. He represented only an exciting moment in time. A *very* exciting moment in time.

And she was no more right for him than he was for her.

He increased the pace, his strokes becoming shorter and his thrusts harder. She clung to him, wrapping her arms and legs tightly around his body as they moved in unison. Harder. Faster. Each stroke delivered exquisite ecstasy. Until torrid passion exploded inside her, and orgasmic convulsions claimed her again and again.

Two more deep thrusts, and hard spasms shuddered through Blake's body as well. No question about it being the most satisfying orgasm he'd ever had. What was there about this woman that touched such a chord inside him? Compulsively organized on the outside, transfixed with only thoughts of planning for the future, yet on the inside, incendiary sex bubbled just beneath the surface, and that part of her had just exploded into delicious release.

He continued to hold her, not wanting to relinquish the feel of her body next to his—a sensation more than mere physical satisfaction.

And he didn't understand why.

****

Vicki awoke alone in Blake's bed. Panic hit her. What had she done? She hurried through a quick shower and dressed, then continued downstairs. Where could he be? And what kind of awkwardness would exist when she saw him? How could she have allowed herself to behave like a wanton slut with a total stranger, regardless of how he made her pulse race?

The smell of fresh coffee greeted her as soon as she reached the bottom of the stairs, but she still didn't see any sign of him. After tending to Ty-Ling's needs with fresh water, food, and a clean litter box, she poured herself a cup of coffee. She stroked the cat's fur and talked to her pet as the feline ate breakfast. "I'm glad you decided to be friends with Blake last night. Digging your claws into him every time he came near you just wouldn't do."

I decided to be friends with Blake last night, too. But will we still be friends this morning?

Vicki took her coffee onto the deck. The early morning air smelled crisp and clean with the sky a brilliant blue. She had never felt as alive as she did right now. A slight frown wrinkled her forehead when she saw clouds gathering on the horizon. The weather forecast told of a storm front moving onshore in the next day or two, an unusual occurrence for this time of year.

A little shiver ran down her spine. Storms meant lightning and thunder. She didn't like them. She remembered the terrible thunderstorms she'd endured as a child when her family lived in various cities in the Midwest. She tried to shrug off a second shiver as she stared down the beach at an approaching jogger.

As the figure drew closer, she recognized Blake. He waved at her, and she returned the gesture. A few moments later, he bounded up the steps to the deck. His breath came in hard gasps, and his skin glistened with a thin sheen of perspiration. He wore jogging shorts and no shirt. Her gaze fixed on his finely honed, well-tanned body. If he jogged on the beach as a daily ritual, then it was no wonder he maintained such a good physique. She could speak from personal experience about his physical condition and stamina. Jogging was not the only thing he did well.

Blake grabbed a towel from the railing and quickly wiped the sweat from his face and neck, then turned his attention to Vicki. "I'm surprised to see you up so early, especially after last night." His voice was light and teasing, but the intensity in his eyes told a different story. "I like to get out at the crack of dawn before anyone else is on the beach."

As it had when she'd appeared in the living room in the middle of the night, her hair hung loose almost to her shoulders. The bangs fringed across her forehead added an extra element of feathery softness to her face. Blake quickly flashed on the image of her hair in wild disarray and her face flushed in the throes of orgasm, a tantalizing vision he knew would remain burned into his memory forever.

He brushed his fingers lightly across her cheek, then threaded them through her hair.

"I like your hair down like this." He quickly withdrew his hand when he saw the pink blush of embarrassment spread across her cheeks. "It suits you."

His thoughts turned to what the next couple of days held for him. Would he have her in his bed again? Had last night been *just one of those things?* A heated moment in time? Two horny people getting it on? He tried to shove away the abstract thought but couldn't quite manage it. The future—that's all he'd heard from Vicki since she arrived, and now his thoughts touched on that very subject. What a strange quirk of fate, the way this woman had appeared at his door and entered his life at a time when he had given up entirely on that very future that so absorbed her.

Her voice cut into his thoughts. "I'm almost always awake with daylight, too. I don't remember the last time I needed to set an alarm to wake up." After taking a sip of coffee, she held up her mug and offered a gracious smile. "This was a pleasant surprise. I smelled the freshly brewed coffee as soon as I came downstairs."

She swept her gaze across the ocean scene in front of her, and a slight furrow creased her brow exhibiting a hint of anxiety he didn't understand.

****

Following breakfast, Vicki walked into the village. Somehow her conversation with Blake had never gotten around to the night before. She hadn't brought it up, and neither had he. Had their lovemaking been only business as usual for him? Granted, she had to accept as much responsibility for their ending up in his bed as he did. The night had started with nothing more than her having the hots for a very sexy man. Would he expect her to continue spending her nights in his bed as long as she lived in his house? Was that his expectation of payment for giving her a temporary place to stay?

The *morning after* hadn't turned out to be what she expected. Neither of them could leave to go home, because they were both already there…at least for the time being. She had never been in this position before, and she wasn't sure how she felt about it. She certainly didn't have any right to make assumptions, nor did she want to do so. She had her life planned out and it didn't have room for a beach bum with no ambition, no matter how sexy or how terrific in bed.

Or, for that matter, how terrific he would be in any other room in the house where they might end up fucking each other senseless.

A quick flash of resignation confirmed for Vicki that last night wouldn't be a one-time thing as far as she was concerned. All he had to do was look at her, and her pussy throbbed with need for his marvelous cock. She was his—body and soul. Well, at least as far as her body was concerned. Her clit still tingled from the expert attention he had lavished on her last night.

But this was a new day, and she had business to conduct. She made the bank her first stop. She walked up to the window where she had purchased the cashier's check, took her copy from her purse, and handed it to the clerk. "I want to know if this has been cashed yet and, if not, what I need to do to cancel it."

She knew it was a futile inquiry, but she needed to try. Her last vestige of hope disappeared when the teller informed her the check had been cashed the previous afternoon, as it turned out within an hour of the time she had given it to Mr. Edwards.

Her next task consisted of checking in with each of her summer clients and giving them Blake's phone number as a temporary contact.

Vicki entered the gift shop and immediately spotted Sally Gaynor stocking shelves in preparation of the opening for the summer season.

"Vicki!" Sally climbed down from the small step ladder. "Just the person I wanted to see."

She withdrew a large envelope from beneath the counter and handed it over. "I have the receipts and records you wanted. The only thing missing is my opening inventory list, but I should have that for you by Monday, along with the employee payroll forms, if that's okay."

"That'll be fine." Vicki surveyed the store. "How are you coming with the grand opening preparations?"

Sally and her husband, Jack, were both school teachers in their late thirties. She taught middle school English, and he taught high school chemistry. They operated the gift shop as a summer business during the school vacation months.

"We're actually ahead of schedule." Sally surveyed the surrounding disarray and laughed. "At least, I think so. Take a good look at this mess."

Vicki and Sally talked for a while longer, and then Vicki continued down the boardwalk until she arrived at a small café. She tried the door but found it locked. Peering through the window, she saw Art Kincaid busy at work. She knocked on the glass to get his attention.

Art unlocked the door and let her in. "Mornin', Vicki."

A retired railroad conductor in his mid-sixties, Art and his wife, Mollie, ran the boardwalk café as a summer only business. They enjoyed the casual, open atmosphere of the beach community and the conversations with tourists.

"Good morning, Art. I'm glad I caught you here." She quickly conducted her business, again giving out Blake's phone number, then continued on her rounds.

Next came a gallery specializing in photographic art. Bob Mason owned the gallery and did all the photography. During the summer, he only accepted photographic assignments that were of particular interest to him. When he needed to be away for a few days on one of those assignments, his mother ran the gallery for him.

The next business on her list was another gift shop, this one dealing exclusively with items associated with the ocean, such as sea shells. A bicycle and roller skate rental shop was number five on her list. The sixth and final summer business she had established as one of her clients was a kite shop. She allowed a brief thought as to the coincidence between that and the fact that Blake apparently liked to fly kites. An omen of some sort? A portent of things to be?

She dismissed those thoughts as illogical. Her business concluded, she returned to the beach house. Enthusiastic shouts reached her ears, telling her something was going on outside. She poured herself a glass of iced tea and carried it out onto the deck.

The voices emanated from a volleyball game next door. Vicki sat on the deck and watched the combatants battle it out. She immediately spotted Blake. Just the sight of his taut muscles and finely honed body sent a tingle of excitement rippling through her pussy.

Each team consisted of one man and two women. She carefully eyed the four women, two of whom wore thongs and the other two string bikinis. They all appeared overly endowed, whether real or implants, she couldn't tell from her vantage point. With the jumping and stretching required to play volleyball, it was a miracle their boobs didn't pop out of their skimpy bikini tops.

She turned her gaze on the two men, with Blake the

best player by far. She allowed a little huff of indignation. He'd obviously gotten lots of practice as he apparently had nothing better to do with his time than play volleyball and fly kites.

The other man was dark haired and in his forties. Blake had told her about his neighbor, Tim, while they were having breakfast. Even though he had not exactly said so, she'd gotten the impression he didn't totally approve of Tim. How odd that an unemployed beach bum would disapprove of a partner in a prestigious law firm.

"That's it. Game!" Tim's shout brought her attention back to the makeshift volleyball court. The winning side consisted of Blake, one blonde woman, and one brunette. Tim's team included another blonde and a redhead. Blake shook hands with Tim and kissed all four women. Not an innocent little peck on the cheek, but a kiss for each one right on the mouth. Even though it appeared to be a quick kiss, had he used his tongue?

The inappropriate thought shocked Vicki. She tried to shove it aside, but became distracted by Blake's blonde teammate rubbing her body against his in obvious invitation.

Tim grabbed the redhead around the waist and lifted her off the sand, burying his face between her ample breasts as he swung her in a circle. She wrapped her legs around his hips and whispered something in his ear. A lascivious expression flashed across his face, and a sly smile curled the corners of his mouth.

He finally put her down and called to his blonde teammate, "Come on, baby. Let's go see what other games we can find inside."

Both women removed their bikini tops, allowing their bare boobs to bounce in the late morning sunlight. Tim reached out and tweaked all four nipples belonging to his two teammates, who were obviously about to become his playmates for sex games. Apparently none of them cared who saw them or knew what they were about to do.

The other blonde continued to hang on Blake while the brunette took off her bikini top. The sunlight glinted off her gold nipple rings as she shimmied in blatant invitation to Blake.

He shot Vicki an apologetic look that seemed to say he'd be there as soon as he could disentangle himself. And again, another inappropriate thought rose to the surface. Had he slept with those two women before? Maybe even as a threesome?

An unexpected and unwanted twinge of jealousy assaulted Vicki's senses, leaving her both surprised and confused. She forced it away as being ludicrous, but it continued to linger at the sidelines of her consciousness.

A moment later, Tim, the redhead, and his blonde teammate disappeared into his house.

Vicki wasn't sure exactly how to read Blake's expression. Should she stay on the deck or make a discreet withdrawal into the house? She had no doubt where Tim and the other two women had gone or what they were going to do. Had they agreed beforehand to have a tryst following the game? It all seemed so sudden to her, so unplanned.

So *spontaneous*.

A strange quiver darted through her body. Her show of spontaneity when she had kissed Blake, ending up in his bed in the middle of the night…that was one thing. But spontaneous sex in the middle of the day? Somehow the thought held a curious fascination for her, fueled even more by the notion that Tim and the two women would be engaged in sex together.

She had tried that once with two men. The idea of sucking on one man's cock while another pumped in and out of her pussy had sounded exciting, but in retrospect she knew one too many margaritas had merely made it seem like a good idea. It had happened many years ago when she was in college, and the three of them had never really gotten coordinated. How much practice did it take for it to stop being awkward and become truly exciting?

Maybe what had passed between Tim and his two companions consisted purely of primal lust rather than heated passion, but it certainly appeared hotter than polite agreement. She transferred her gaze from the volleyball court to the ocean as her thoughts drifted back to Blake. To the memory of his hard cock buried deep inside her. To the torrid sensations that exploded inside her when he'd sucked her clit into his mouth. Just the memory caused her pussy to throb. She closed her eyes and squirmed uncomfortably in her chair.

"Hi."

Blake's deep voice interrupted her thoughts, and it was just as well, because those thoughts had turned to the unsettling desires that came over her whenever he was near. He stood next to the deck, looking up at her while using the outdoor shower to rinse off the sand.

Vicki glanced toward the blonde and brunette slowly making their way down the beach away from Tim's house. "Where are your friends going?"

"Beats me. Maybe to find another volleyball game. When did you get back?"

"About half an hour ago. I've just been enjoying the sun and watching your game."

"Oh?" He eyed her intently. "Did you have half an hour marked off in your schedule book for nothing more than simple enjoyment?" A mischievous grin played at the corners of his mouth. "Not a very efficient use of your time, if you ask me."

Blake knew the remark was uncalled for, but her statement had been in such contrast to her clearly voiced philosophy, and he couldn't help it. He noted the way she immediately bristled. Of course, the heated and surprising sex they had engaged in last night was also in contrast to her well-voiced philosophy. But when she had seemed to prefer avoiding any conversation about it at breakfast…well, he wasn't sure what she thought, what he should say, or where things stood between them. So he had followed her example and hadn't mentioned it.

"I'll have you know—"

"Why didn't you come over and join us? There's always room for one more." He grabbed the towel from the railing and quickly dried off. "Do you play volleyball?"

"I played a little in gym class when I was in high school, but I've never played beach volleyball." She glanced down at the sand. A hint of embarrassment darted across her features. She dropped her voice to a near whisper. "I would have been in the way, would have slowed up the game. I'm not very athletic."

"Really?" He leveled a questioning look in her direction. His voice held a teasing quality. "I wouldn't say that. You seem very athletic and coordinated to me."

An immediate blush spread across her cheeks. There it was again, that almost painfully shy manner that would occasionally escape from behind her ultra-organized façade, which also hid the hottest partner who had provided him with the most incredible night of sex he had experienced in a long time...perhaps ever. He looked at her for a moment, wondering what was going on in her head.

"If I give you enough notice, maybe schedule the event far enough in advance, would you like to join in the game next time?" It was as much a challenge as a question.

"I don't think so." Vicki tried to keep her tone all business so she wouldn't give away her thoughts. "I'm sure the other players wouldn't want their game slowed down by a novice."

No question in her mind, he was baiting her. She refused to succumb to the tactic she suspected was just another attempt on his part to deter her from her chosen goals. He had made several such references, and she had become accustomed to them. He had his philosophy and she had hers—polar opposites with perspectives on life that simply did not fit together in any way. The only thing about them that did fit together was his cock and her pussy.

And they fit together perfectly.

The nagging pull of her instincts told her Blake was a very dangerous man to be around. Not dangerous in a physical sense, but most certainly an emotional one. She took a large swallow of her iced tea, as if to signal the end to her wandering thoughts. Regardless of how hot the sex had been, he remained as far removed from her concept of the ideal man as anyone could be. She forced her thoughts to more sensible matters as she rose from the deck chair.

"I checked with the bank. Mr. Edwards cashed the check about an hour after I gave it to him. I imagine…" She took a calming breath, then swallowed down the lump in her throat. "I imagine that pretty well speaks for itself. But just in case, I'll give the rental office a call on the off chance that someone might be there. I need to get myself situated somewhere so I can unpack my boxes and set up my office.

"I can't continue with this unsettled feeling, and it certainly isn't fair to you. I'm sure my presence has hampered your daily activities." She glanced toward the volleyball court and thought about Tim with those two women. Would Blake be engaged in sex games with the other two if she hadn't been here? "I've certainly intruded into your social life."

"No, you haven't." Blake flashed on the scene of Tim headed inside with the two women and wondered if that had anything to do with Vicki's comment. Having been in Tim's playroom, he didn't have any doubts about the activities happening inside his neighbor's house at the moment. The only real question was whether he'd also be in Tim's playroom if Vicki hadn't returned from the village much sooner than he'd thought she would and if he hadn't spotted her sitting on his deck. Or would the memory of last night have kept him from engaging in mindless sex with women who didn't mean anything more to him than providing a place to poke his dick?

The more he thought about it, the more he came to

the realization that he would have declined the obvious invitation from the blonde and returned to his own house whether or not Vicki had returned from the village.

She nervously brushed at an imaginary loose tendril of hair. "I'd better make that phone call." She hurried inside.

Blake watched her with curiosity, an increased intensity, and heated desire burning deep inside him. She definitely didn't have anything in common with the type of women he'd been fucking for the last two years. Uptight and overly organized was *not* what he looked for in a woman. His choices had revolved around women wanting as little conversation as possible, so he could take them straight to bed. He didn't need anyone special in his life, not anymore. He couldn't afford the emotional investment a true relationship required. He couldn't risk the pain if it didn't work out.

He turned his gaze toward the horizon, noticing the storm clouds gathering in the distance. But as much as he tried to force his thoughts on something else, they kept returning to Vicki and the night they'd spent together in his bed.

He shook his head. He couldn't allow his thoughts to travel in that direction. He wouldn't be able to handle losing someone a second time. Someone who gave purpose and meaning to his life. Someone who made it a joy just to greet each new day and wonder what marvelous things it would bring. Someone who could be as much an intricate part of his life as his son had been.

A very special someone who could be the one to make his shattered life whole again.

Chapter Four

Vicki disconnected the call and replaced the handset in the charger. Her attempt to reach the rental agency had not been answered, not even by their answering service. Disappointment coursed through her. It only reinforced her fear that she would never see her money again. It also told her emphatically that she needed to find another place to live...and quickly.

The loss of her money would set back her plans for her master's degree, but there was little she could do about that problem at the moment. It also meant she would need to find a full time job after she completed her obligation to her summer clients. She allowed a heavy sigh of disappointment. All of her perfect plans had been totally destroyed.

Suddenly she felt very alone and lost.

In an attempt to shake off her sadness, Vicki took the morning newspaper to the kitchen table and turned to the classified ads. With pen in hand, she carefully went over each and every rental listing.

An hour passed, and she had still not found a single ad to pursue. The only ones that suited her needs were far too expensive. She never should have sold her car. She never should have paid the entire five months rental in advance. She never should have...so many things she thought she had carefully planned out but never should have done.

And among them, having hot sex with Blake neared the top of the list. Not that she regretted it. In fact, it had been the best sex of her life. But that didn't change the fact that she shouldn't have done it. Even though neither of them had mentioned their tryst so far that morning, it made walking away that much more difficult.

She could still taste his kiss. Just the memory of their lovemaking sent dampness to her panties. Her pussy purred with satisfaction and at the same time wanted more. She couldn't allow his offer of temporary shelter for the weekend to be anything more than that— temporary. And that brief time frame ended tomorrow evening when the owner of the house returned to confirm what she already knew—Blake had the legal right to the house. She stared at the open newspaper and all the house rental ads she had circled and then crossed out.

Blake stood on the deck looking through the sliding glass door at Vicki in the kitchen. She shoved the newspaper aside, despair etched on her face. He thought of his son and of the future he had put on hold two years ago. Once again, she touched that vulnerable spot he had tried to bury, a spot he thought had died along with his son.

On the surface, it appeared to everyone that he enjoyed the events of day-to-day carefree fun. But no matter how hard he tried, he hadn't been able to fool himself. His life had become empty with something very important missing. He couldn't explain it. He couldn't even translate the feeling into conscious thought, let alone words, but it was something akin to a need to be involved in life. To once again have someone with whom he could share his days, someone who would give his life purpose and direction. Vicki had managed to awaken that place inside him, and he found it very disturbing. This compulsively ordered woman was not who he needed.

Blake forced the thoughts away and went inside the house. "Are you okay? You look like you're about to burst into tears."

"What?" Her head jerked up. "Oh…yes, I'm fine. I was just looking at the rental ads." She placed her hand on the folded newspaper. "There wasn't anything listed that suits my needs. Actually, there were two, but one was twice what I can afford, and the other requires me to have a car. Until I get my money back from Mr. Edwards…" She paused as if trying to gather her thoughts. "Well, don't worry. I'll find some other arrangement by Monday so you won't be inconvenienced any longer. I'm sure he'll refund my money."

Blake poured himself a glass of iced tea and took a long swig before answering her, even though she had not asked a question. "We'll tackle your Mr. Edwards first thing Monday morning and see what he has to say for himself. Gary Sanderson will be home tomorrow night, and I'm sure he can help straighten out this mess and see that you get your money back."

He downed the rest of his iced tea. "Meanwhile…" He set the empty glass on the counter. "I've got a kite to get up in the air." He looked at her for a moment, then an idea struck him. "I was going to hook some of my stunt kites together and fly them. There's a nice stiff breeze out, but…" He offered her an encouraging smile. "Have you ever flown a kite?"

What a frivolous waste of time. Vicki had things to do. She should be doing…doing *what?* It suddenly struck her that without being able to unpack her belongings and set up her office, she was very limited in how much work she could do. "Flying kites? Isn't that more the type of thing children do?"

It was certainly not a mature activity an adult should be engaged in, especially someone like Blake who was so adept at *other* activities.

He shot her an appraising look. "Not at all. There are kite flying championships everywhere with adults as the participants rather than kids. In fact, there's a kite shop in the village. You could check there and find information on the contest held here every June. People come from all over the country to compete for major prizes. I'm thinking about entering this year."

She couldn't hide her surprise. "A kite flying contest?"

"Come on." Blake grabbed her hand and pulled her up. He hesitated for a moment, then folded her into his embrace.

They hadn't talked about what had happened last night, but the experience and excitement had dominated his thoughts from the moment he woke. The passion of the night had been immediately resurrected this morning when he'd gazed at her nude body sleeping in his bed. He had even allowed a fleeting thought about what it would be like to wake each morning and find her next to him, but had quickly shoved the impractical—and emotionally frightening—notion from his mind.

He lowered his mouth to hers, a kiss that started gently at first before escalating along with the desire coursing through his body. It was as if neither of them had a need to talk about what had happened.

And what seemed to be happening again.

She slipped her arms around his neck and returned his kiss, her passion matching his spark for spark. He flicked his tongue at her lower lip, then penetrated the recesses of her mouth. She answered his advance by rubbing her belly against his erection the same way the blonde had after the volleyball game. Unlike his actions with the blonde, this time he responded enthusiastically.

He cupped her ass cheeks and pulled her tightly against his lower body, grinding his pelvis against hers. He broke off the kiss only long enough to whisper in her ear. "Let's go upstairs."

"Yes." She managed only the one ragged word.

Nothing else needed to be said. They quickly ascended the stairs. It took only a minute for their discarded clothing to land on the floor. The sounds of their labored breathing filled the air.

Vicki stretched out on Blake's bed. He turned, straddled her shoulders, and stretched his torso down the length of her prone body. Wrapping his arms around her hips, he cupped her ass cheeks and plastered his mouth to her juicy pussy. He found himself quickly immersed in the addictive taste that belonged to her alone. He flicked his tongue in and out of her opening, then sucked her engorged clit into his mouth.

Her moans of delight fed his need as he continued to feast on her delicious taste. No woman had ever imprinted her essence on him the way she had. A taste, a scent…would he ever have his fill? His thoughts came to an abrupt halt when her lips suddenly closed around his cockhead, then slid up and down his rigid shaft.

His groan vibrated from the place where his mouth touched Vicki's clit. The sensation continued to reverberate through her body, pushing her into what she knew from the previous night's experience would be the first of many fantastic orgasms. Each of his sucking motions sent her rushing toward the ultimate release. Her entire body quivered with sexual arousal so intense it left her breathless.

His mouth…his tongue…they were only part of his display of unparalleled talent. She floated on a cloud of euphoria. Throbbed to a primal beat. Every nerve ending in her body tingled with excitement. Then the first orgasmic wave crashed through her. A quick pelvic thrust, then her entire body convulsed in delicious, heart-pounding ecstasy.

Myriad conflicting thoughts ripped through her mind. Blake was wrong for her in every way that mattered. A kite flying beach bum. An unemployed playboy with no sense of responsibility. Orgasmic contractions seized control of her senses, banishing any further thought. And each intensely erotic ripple had her sucking in more of his shaft.

Her taste filled Blake's mouth. Her body acted on him much like an addictive drug. The more he had, the more he wanted. The more he wanted, the more he needed. No, he'd never have his fill of her. But what did it mean and where was it leading? Her hips bucked erratically, shoving her pussy hard against his mouth. He nibbled at her clit, totally losing himself in her as she continued to work her mouth along his stiff cock.

The churning in his balls spoke to him, screaming out his need for release. He momentarily gave up her tasty pussy and reached for a condom packet. A minute later, he stretched out on his back with her straddling his hips. He gripped her waist and lowered her onto his sheathed cock. The look of exquisite rapture that covered her face sent a hard rush through him. Her eyes glowed with the same hot passion that coursed through his veins. She leaned forward, her breasts coming to rest in his hands, her tautly puckered nipples pressed into his palms.

Blake didn't know how much longer he could hold out. Her inner muscles clenched around his shaft, tugging and squeezing with a unique rhythm that quickly drove him to the edge. He had never had his cock in a hotter nest or one that felt as good. One that felt as if he really belonged there. One that felt like home.

One that felt like a lifetime.

The unwanted thought disappeared as hard spasms shuddered through his body. He squeezed her breasts in time with her orgasmic contractions, which drained his balls of all he had to offer. Her body went limp, falling forward against his chest. He wrapped his arms around her, allowing one hand to glide down her back and come to rest on her perfectly rounded ass. Playing his fingers along the crevice separating her cheeks, he fought to bring his breathing under control and restore some semblance of reason back to the moment.

They hadn't talked about last night, but he knew they had to talk about it now. He couldn't pretend nothing important had happened, that she represented nothing different from any other hot fuck that might come his way. She was different all right. Unique. Special.

Very special.

He smoothed her hair away from her damp face. "Vicki, we need to talk about—"

"No." She placed her fingertips against his lips. "Please don't make more of this than it is. I want you to know I'm not in the habit of falling into bed with every man I meet, with men I've only known a few hours. You and I...we don't have anything in common. Our lifestyles and goals are completely different, but there's obviously something about our body chemistry, something pulling us—"

Now it was Blake's turn to place his fingertips against her lips to stop her words. "I never thought for a moment that you promiscuously hopped into bed with every man who crossed your path. If you don't want to talk about this right now, we can wait until—"

Vicki stopped his words with a kiss. Even though it felt strange with neither of them mentioning what had happened the night before, she didn't want to confront the truth. Didn't want to deal with where it could lead. Two ships passing in the night. As different as could be in what they wanted from life...except in bed where they both wanted the exact same thing. To fuck each other into exhaustion and satisfy every carnal desire. The best thing to do was simply leave it at that. Accept it for what it was—two people with an incredible case of the hots for each other and nothing more. A short term situation with no long term consequences to consider.

At least, that's what she wanted to believe. She couldn't allow a thought to the contrary. No way would she entertain the possibility of anything more with this man. She had her entire future planned out, and he absolutely did not fit into that plan. Nothing about him fit into her life even though everything about his body fit with hers.

"We have to talk about this, Vicki. Not now, apparently, but sometime soon. This is too hot. Too all consuming. Much too…"

****

Blake stepped onto the deck, closing the door behind him when he remembered the cat was loose somewhere in the house. He stared at the storm clouds on the horizon, his thoughts lost in a confused swirl that revolved around Vicki. She tried so hard to be tough and independent in spite of her terrible predicament, and each attempt made him more aware of how much he wanted to take care of her.

"I guess I'm ready." Her voice sounded more like someone being led to an unavoidable ordeal rather than a person enthusiastically participating in a fun activity.

She stepped onto the deck, and he turned to face her. She had pulled on a simple pale blue T-shirt that caressed the soft curve of her breasts and a pair of dark blue shorts. A sharp jab of desire attacked him. It had been less than an hour since they'd showered together after generating enough heat to nearly set the sheets on fire. Yet, just the sight of her made him want to carry her off to bed all over again, as if he hadn't had sex in months.

It had taken a bit of convincing for him to get her to agree to a kite flying lesson. She kept using the words *frivolous* and *waste of time*. Although totally uninhibited in bed, she continued to vacillate between being uptight and guarded when dealing with innocent fun.

He quickly regained his composure, then stooped to pick up the box kite. In spite of the stiff breeze, it would be the easiest for her to fly. "Come on, let's get away from the house." He led her out onto the sand and held the kite toward her. "Here, give it a try."

"What do I do?" She looked at him with reluctant eyes, making no effort to take the kite.

"Hold the kite in your left hand and the string in your right, like this." He moved behind her and reached around to show her how to handle the kite and string. His body brushed her back as he guided her hands. Warmth washed through him at the momentary physical contact. He hoped his voice didn't sound as unsteady as he felt. "Let out a little of the string and run along the beach until the wind catches the kite, then continue to let out the string until it's flying high."

He stepped away from her and offered her an encouraging smile. "There's nothing to it."

Vicki hesitantly took the kite from him, handling it in an awkward manner. Tremors raced through her body the moment he'd stepped behind her. What was she doing? What was this insanity she had allowed herself to be drawn into? Kite flying? She should be doing something productive to occupy her time until she could get her office set up and start work. Something like…well, she couldn't think of anything specific at the moment. Her mind touched briefly on the time they'd spent indulging their carnal desires. An immediate ripple raced through her pussy, as if she hadn't had sex in months rather than having just been completely and deliciously satisfied.

She dug her feet into the sand to get a firm footing. The fine granules squished between her toes as she started to run. The wind caught the kite and pulled it sharply upward. The hard tug on the string came as a surprise. Following Blake's instructions, she let it out. Her heartbeat increased along with her excitement as she watched the colorful kite rise into the sky.

Then it faltered and crashed to the sand, the thrill of the moment gone. Disappointment enveloped her, a totally unexpected reaction, which caught her off guard.

"Oh, no." She looked at Blake, who'd been running along the beach beside her. "Have I broken it?"

"No, it's okay." He reeled in the string and picked up the kite, handing it back to her. He offered an encouraging smile. "Here, try it again. Only this time, let the string out a little more slowly."

Vicki was not sure why she had agreed to try it the first time and now she was about to try it again. What a silly activity, running along the sand towing a box made out of fiberglass rods and brightly colored nylon fabric. She accepted the kite and string from him, took a calming breath, and began to run. The sharp tug on the string confirmed the wind had taken hold of the kite.

Blake kept pace with her, shouting encouragement as they ran down the beach. "That's it, Vicki. Good. Now, slowly let out the string. Make sure the line stays taut."

She slowed her pace and carefully let out the string. This time, the kite rose higher and higher into the air until she had let out the entire length.

The wind tried to pull it from her hands with a hard tug along the string. She turned her face upward and watched the colorful box kite flying in the breeze. She laughed like a child enjoying the carefree arena of play...the excitement of innocent fun. The heavy burden of responsibility she chose to carry on her shoulders like a mantle had lifted for the moment.

"That's perfect." His genuine enthusiasm for her accomplishment echoed in his voice. "You've got it."

"Look. It's actually flying!" She radiated the excitement that filled her almost to overflowing. But her elation quickly disappeared when she took a couple of steps backward and lost her footing. She stumbled and fell. The kite yanked the string from her grasp. They both watched it soar away over the rooftops and out of sight.

Blake's robust laughter filled the air as he moved to help her up from where she lay sprawled on the beach. "That's an undignified position for someone so proper."

He reached out his hand. She refused the offer and quickly scrambled to her feet, not sure whether to be embarrassed or angry at him for making fun of her. Anger won out, if for no other reason than to cover her embarrassment. She turned an indignant gaze on him. "I'd appreciate it if you'd refrain from laughing at me."

She brushed sand from her clothes and legs, then turned toward the house.

"Hold on. You missed a spot." Blake brushed his hand across her rear. "You had a little sand on your caboose."

The heat rose on her cheeks and across the back of her neck. She glanced around to determine if anyone had seen what he did, then shot him one last angry barb. "It wasn't my idea to be out here doing something this ridiculous."

She stomped off through the soft sand as best she could. But more prominent in her mind than losing his kite and being embarrassed and angry was the tantalizing sensation of his hand brushing her ass. Desire once again flooded her mind and body.

Confusion ran rampant inside her head. He was wrong for her in every way, lifestyles as different as could be. Yet every encounter with Blake Callahan, regardless of how fleeting or innocent, left her trembling with desire. He consumed her thoughts.

"Hey, Vicki. Come on back. I'm not laughing at you. It's the situation that's funny."

She glanced over her shoulder in time to see him start after her.

"Vicki...wait a minute."

Tears burned her eyes. She wiped them away with the back of her hand. He had humiliated her by forcing her into that undignified situation. She had to get away from him and find another place to live, this afternoon if at all possible. The thought that he hadn't forced her to try flying the kite, hadn't been responsible for her losing her footing in the sand and falling, nor had he actually humiliated her, managed to gain access to her brain before she forced it away. The true reason she needed to get away from him had nothing to do with that and everything to do with her physical desire for him, something that excited her in the sensual pleasure it gave her and, at the same time, frightened her in the overwhelming loss of control it represented.

"I don't understand why you're mad." Blake caught up with her at the deck and took hold of her arm just long enough to bring her to a halt. He extended a teasing grin. "After all, it was my kite that flew away, and I'm not mad."

"I'll pay for the damn kite." She yanked open the

sliding door and stepped inside the house, but he stayed right behind her.

"Don't be ridiculous. There's no reason for you to pay for the kite." He tried to grab her arm again, but she jerked away in an attempt to put some distance between them.

Vicki didn't know what to do. She wanted to run and hide from her own growing emotions for Blake. Sex was one thing. She wanted him physically more than she had ever wanted anyone. He fulfilled her every need on a level she had never before experienced. But she hadn't thought her emotions would ever become involved. When she first encountered him, she immediately recognized him as an emotionally dangerous man, but she had no idea just how dangerous until this moment. He made her feel things she didn't want to feel, things she didn't have time for at this point in her carefully planned out life. He made her question her own philosophy and carefully honed beliefs.

"Come on." He held out his hand and offered her an encouraging smile. "Let's try it again. I have lots of kites that need to be taken out and given some fresh air."

"No, I think I've had enough kite flying for the day." She projected a formal attitude and a firm voice as she tried to quell the nervousness churning in her stomach. The thrill she had experienced when the kite tugged against the string as it rose into the air sent a tremor of excitement racing through her body. She steeled her determination. Kite flying—irresponsible and unacceptable. A frivolous activity that didn't have a place in her carefully scheduled life. Everything about this man was wrong for her—a truth she needed to keep telling herself.

Everything was wrong, except for the way he made her feel.

Vicki quickly retreated to her room, closed the door, and did her best to avoid Blake for the rest of the afternoon. Later, she walked back into the village and spent a considerable amount of time browsing at the bookstore, finally purchasing two paperbacks she'd been meaning to read. She checked the bulletin board at the local market to see if there were any *For Rent* ads that had not been in the newspaper, then wandered the streets looking in the windows of various shops. A sign in the window of the kite shop advertised the upcoming competition Blake had mentioned. She hadn't noticed it when she'd been there earlier to meet with her client.

All the while, she kept a wary eye on the dark clouds and a tight rein on the anxieties caused by the approaching storm.

The temperature dropped. Her shorts and T-shirt weren't warm enough for the cool evening air. She needed to return to the beach house soon to tend to Ty-Ling's dinner. She couldn't stay away any longer, or go the entire evening without having at least some contact with Blake. But she would try. She would retire to her room early and read. No doubt existed in her mind— this man posed a real threat to her neatly ordered life. But in much the same manner as the moth being drawn to the dangerous flame...

****

Blake stood just inside the sliding glass door sipping his morning coffee as he watched the dark storm clouds moving onshore and the wind whipping up white caps on the ocean. The only apparent life on the broad expanse of beach was a large brown dog slowly making its way along the edge of the water, pausing occasionally to sniff at something then continuing on its leisurely course. Blake had dressed in jeans and a sweatshirt to ward off the chill in the air. No one would be flying kites or playing beach volleyball for a while, not until the storm moved on.

He had been disappointed by Vicki's decision to retire to her room right after dinner last night. He had stayed up hoping she would come back downstairs to watch television or even get something from the kitchen, but she hadn't. Several times he had thought about going to her room, but he didn't want her to think his only interest or concern with her was how many times he could fuck her. True, he didn't seem to be able to get enough of her. But sex was far removed from being his only interest in her.

Very far removed.

His thoughts turned to their kite flying lesson and their brief time of carefree enjoyment. He had lots of kites. He had purchased the first one for his son when the boy was three, and Blake had taken much delight in teaching Bobby to fly it. It was probably why he still flew kites. They were a link with his son, with the father and son activity they had most enjoyed together. He remembered the delight he'd seen on his boy's face every time a kite lifted into the air. The same look of excitement that had covered Vicki's face when the kite caught the wind, a look he wanted to see again. A feeling he wanted to recapture and share with her.

"Good morning."

Blake started at the sound of Vicki's voice, then turned to face her. She had dressed in a pair of worn jeans and a lightweight sweater. She wore her hair down, framing her face in a soft swirl of luxurious chestnut. A hint of a russet color dotted her lips and looked so very tempting. His heart instantly filled with the warm feeling that moved through him whenever he was around her. The momentary excitement she had shown when flying the kite filled his senses with an emotional contentment he had not felt in quite some time.

"Good morning, yourself." Blake didn't like the surprising hint of huskiness that tinged his voice. "You…uh…went to bed early last night. Are you feeling okay?" He self-consciously shifted his weight from one foot to the other. "Or was it something I said?"

He reached out and lightly touched his fingertips to her cheek, then quickly withdrew his hand. He suddenly felt awkward, not sure what to say or whether he should have even alluded to the previous day's disagreement. A strange situation, especially considering the hot and heavy way they had indulged their sexual desires in the short time she'd been in the house.

"There's fresh coffee." He motioned toward the kitchen and extended an uncertain smile. Then he glanced out the door. "Looks like we're in for quite a rainstorm."

Vicki already had a vigilant eye on the approaching clouds. She still felt a little guilty about purposefully avoiding Blake the previous afternoon and evening. Upon reflection, she knew she had over reacted to his teasing, which had combined with her own amazement over the unexpected joy she had experienced when the kite lifted into the air.

She tried to blame her unacceptable behavior on her trepidation over the impending storm. But it didn't do any good. Even though the storm caused her anxiety, it hadn't been responsible for her rudeness. Too many changes swirled around her, too much she had not anticipated. Things were happening too fast. She feared she had lost all control over her life and didn't know how to get it back.

She tried to project a casual manner. "I see you have the fireplace going. The aroma of fresh coffee is always good. But when you add the scent of burning logs...well, I don't know which smells better."

"There's something about a cool, stormy-looking day that calls for a fire." Blake turned toward the kitchen to refill his nearly empty coffee mug. The sound of the doorbell stopped him in mid-stride. His brow furrowed in a quick hint of confusion.

"I wonder who that could be," he glanced at the clock, "at seven-thirty on a Sunday morning."

Blake opened the door and greeted the owners of the beach house with surprise. "Gary. Jennifer. Come in."

"Sorry to stop by so early, but we were just on our way home. We decided to drive back into town before the storm hit. I saw the smoke coming out of the chimney and knew you were awake. I wanted to make a quick check on the repair of the sliding glass door. This storm is predicted to be a real blow-out, and I don't want it to leak or..." Gary Sanderson's gaze landed on Vicki. He shot Blake a curious look. "Are we interrupting?"

"Not at all." Blake extended a gracious smile. "Jennifer and Gary Sanderson, this is Victoria

Templeton." He turned toward Vicki. "Gary and Jennifer own the house." He gave Vicki a quick wink and a comforting smile. "How's this for perfect timing? It saves us from having to make that phone call."

"It's a pleasure to meet you." Vicki extended her hand toward the early morning guests.

Gary shook her hand while shooting Blake another quizzical look. "A phone call?" His voice held the teasing quality that usually permeated their conversations. "Don't tell me you're going to be one of those impossibly demanding tenants."

"*We...*" He gestured toward Vicki. "We, uh, have a problem. Let's sit down and have some coffee while Vicki explains her plight."

Gary, Jennifer, Vicki, and Blake settled in at the dining room table. Gary cast another curious look at Blake, then eyed Vicki before returning his attention to Blake. "What seems to be the problem?"

"It appears that Vicki has been swindled out of five months' rent by the agent who had this house listed as rental property."

"A rental agent?" Gary's eyes widened in shock, the same shock surrounding his words. A stunned expression covered Gary's face. "I took this property away from that agency two months ago when it changed ownership. I didn't like the man who took over the business." Gary turned toward Vicki, his brow furrowed. "You paid someone five months' rent for this house? Who were you dealing with? Tell me what happened."

Chapter Five

"Are you all right?" Blake placed his hand on Vicki's shoulder. Half an hour had gone by since Gary and Jennifer departed.

Vicki looked up at him from where she sat on the couch. "How could this have happened?" She couldn't hide the despair in her soft voice.

"Like Gary suggested, I think you should call the police and file a report."

"But what if there's a logical explanation? Perhaps Mr. Edwards got sick and had to go home. I'd hate to get the police involved if it was an honest mistake." She knew she was grasping at straws. Facts were facts. No way would she ever see her money again.

"Even if Mr. Edwards has a legitimate reason for not returning your calls, you heard what Gary said. Mr. Edwards had no legal right to rent this house. The listing had been taken away from him two months ago."

Hopelessness washed over her as she accepted the reality she could no longer deny or ignore. "How could I have been so foolish as to have actually paid the entire five months in advance?"

"Don't blame yourself." Blake sat next to her and pulled her into his arms. "You couldn't have known he would do this or have any reason to suspect him of wrong-doing."

He cradled her head against his shoulder. A

shudder moved through her body. She slipped her arms around his waist and clung to him, seeking his support.

"I thought it odd when he told me the owners required it, but that rental agency has always had a good reputation so I never questioned it. I didn't realize it had changed ownership."

"As Gary said, that was the reason he took the property rental away from them. Mr. Edwards must have kept a key to the house when Gary terminated their agreement. I wonder how many other people Mr. Edwards has scammed. My guess is that he won't be at the office in the morning, or any other morning, for that matter. He's probably skipped town."

"Yes...I..." A sob caught in her throat as she tried to keep her anguish under control. "I think you're right." Tears welled in her eyes and threatened to trickle down her cheeks. The last thing she wanted was for him to see her cry. All her life she had always been in control. She considered herself to be strong and capable. Now everything in her life seemed to be crumbling around her. She felt totally helpless, the sensation decidedly uncomfortable and unfamiliar.

She quickly blinked away the tears and took a calming breath. "Well..." She eased back from his embrace and stood. "I guess I'd better figure out what to do. Tomorrow's the day I'm supposed to start setting up the books and business records for my clients. I need to find a place to work and live for the summer. I guess..." She took another deep breath, but it didn't do anything to settle the tremors spreading through her body. "I'll just have to take the money from my college fund and put off getting my master's degree." Sadness crept into her voice. "Looks like it will take me a lot longer than I had planned."

"Wait, don't be so hasty. Let's talk about this." Blake took hold of her hand and gently tugged on it until they were both seated on the couch again. He placed his hands on her shoulders, turned her toward him, and slowly worked his fingers against her tight muscles. As his fingertips kneaded her flesh, he plumbed the depths of her hazel eyes. The sharp emotional pull at that place buried deep inside him was as much a worry as a reality.

"First, we need to unpack your boxes and get you settled in. You said you'd planned on using the dining room as an office. I don't have any problem with that. You should probably order your own phone line, though, for business."

"I...I don't understand." Confusion filled her eyes. "What—"

"I'm suggesting you stay here for the summer. We obviously have very different philosophies on life, but I believe we can co-exist in this house without interfering with each other's needs." He tried to suppress the grin playing across his lips without much success. "Even the furry little beast has stopped inflicting pain and suffering on me."

Again, as it had originally happened, the suggestion spontaneously burst forth from the place inside him she had now thoroughly invaded. He had not given it conscious consideration, and neither had he evaluated the situation...or the possible consequences.

"But...but what about the—"

"Don't tell me you're going to make another list of pros and cons." He extended a wry grin to let her know he was kidding, then turned serious once again. "I'll tell you what we'll do. After you set up your office, we'll go next door and talk to Tim Flannigan about what steps you need to take to get your money back. Maybe he wouldn't mind providing a little free legal advice…one volleyball buddy to another, so to speak."

Vicki held his gaze and allowed him to draw her into his embrace. He brushed his lips lightly against her forehead, stood, and tugged on her hand to urge her to her feet.

"Come on, Vicki. Let's get your boxes moved into the dining room so you can set up your office. Then we'll go next door and talk to Tim."

She rose and followed him.

****

Tim's surprise at seeing Blake and Vicki at his door registered on his face. Blake made the introductions.

"Victoria Templeton, this is indeed a pleasure." Tim pressed his lips to the back of her hand while proffering a courtly bow. His dark eyes sparkled with some hidden inner meaning. "I didn't realize Blake had such a charming roommate."

"It's nothing like that." Blake moved quickly to counter Tim's assumption. "It's simply a temporary arrangement of convenience. What Vicki needs is a little legal advice if you don't mind."

"For this lovely lady, whatever she needs." No way could anyone mistake the lascivious twinkle in Tim's eyes as he raked his gaze slowly up and down her body. He put his arm around her shoulders and steered her toward the couch in his living room. "Now, pretty lady, you sit right here and tell Uncle Timmy all about your problem."

His immediate familiarity and condescending tone set her teeth on edge. She did not like the way he touched her or the knowing look in his eyes. She edged away from him, trying to put a businesslike distance between them without offending him. She glanced at Blake. His expression clearly showed his unhappiness about something, but she didn't know what.

"Well, Tim…" She shifted a little farther away. "It appears I've been swindled by the agency that rented me Blake's house." She went on to fill him in on all the details, including her verification that the check had been cashed. "I need to know what steps to take to get my money back. Should I file a police report?"

"Ah, yes. You do seem to have a bit of a sticky problem." Tim reached over and stroked her cheek.

Vicki backed away and batted at his hand. "I'd rather you didn't do that."

"Sorry. I didn't mean to upset you." He studied her for a moment, then flashed a practiced smile. "Let's hold off on calling the police until we've made an attempt to contact your Mr. Edwards directly rather than leaving messages with the answering service. I'll write him a letter requesting the immediate return of your money, throwing in a couple of things about his operating in bad faith and our being prepared to take more drastic steps if the matter isn't resolved in a timely manner. We'll see if that will be enough to do it. Now, do you have his business card? I'll need that and copies of any documents he gave you, such as a receipt for your payment and a signed rental agreement."

She handed Tim the file folder containing a copy she had made of the rental agreement and cashier's check receipt, along with the agency's business card.

"Are you sure I shouldn't file a police report? After all, what he did is illegal since he didn't have permission to represent the property...fraud or something."

"I think you should hold off until I've made an attempt to reach him. If this can be settled without going to court, it will be easier all around."

She maintained a strictly business attitude in spite of his smooth yet shark-like predatory manner. "How much is your fee for handling this?"

"Now, don't you worry your pretty little head about that." He practically leered at her. "Let me get the letter written first, then we'll see where we go from there." He leaned forward and tried to slip his arm around her shoulders, his voice a throaty whisper. "I'm sure we can work something out."

Vicki bristled at his unwelcome advance, abruptly jumped to her feet, and took a couple of steps away from the couch.

"I'm not asking you for free legal services, something we can *work out later*." A hint of irritation crept into her voice before she could stop it. "I expect this to be a strictly business arrangement."

"I'll get someone in my office on this first thing in the morning. Hopefully we'll have a response by the end of the week. That will give us a little extra something to celebrate at my party on Saturday." Tim rose, took her hand in his, and cupped her elbow with his other hand as he walked her to the door. "You will come to the party, won't you?"

"I'll have to check my schedule." A knot tightened in the pit of her stomach.

"Thanks for your help, Tim." Blake cut him off and steered Vicki out the door.

As soon as they were away from Tim's house, Blake let go of her arm. He had been watching and listening to Tim, and he didn't like what he'd seen and heard. Tim had blatantly hit on Vicki, as if she were one of his vacuous beach bunnies with the silicone boobs. And Tim had done it in front of him, knowing full well she was staying at his house. Granted, he had tried to make it clear to Tim that nothing was going on between Vicki and him, but still…

A sudden need to protect her, to take care of her, welled inside him and took control of his actions. "Tim's a fun guy and has a reputation as a sharp attorney, but I don't trust him personally. Watch yourself around him."

He carefully eyed her. This compulsively organized woman didn't have the type of experience necessary to handle a slick operator like Tim. He knew it to be true in spite of the heated passion Blake had shared with her and the way she'd clearly demonstrated superior skill and talent in the bedroom. The idea of Tim treating Vicki as if she were nothing more than one of the many women who participated in his playroom orgies left Blake both angry and confused. "In fact, I think you should just stay away from him."

"Excuse me?" She stopped and stared at Blake in disbelief. "Do I understand you correctly? Are you attempting to tell me how to conduct myself and telling me who I should and should not see? You're trying to run my life? I'll have you know I'm perfectly capable of taking care of myself. You have no right to dictate my activities or my companions."

"Wait a minute." Her sudden outburst surprised him. "I was only looking out for your well-being."

"I can look out for it myself. I've been doing it ever since I graduated from high school. I'm a divorced woman who put herself through college, and I've managed to get along just fine without any outside interference."

A sudden shiver darted through Vicki. She blamed part of the reason on the cool, damp breeze associated with the approaching storm. But the rest of it? Undoubtedly an emotional reaction to the proprietary nature of Blake's comments. She certainly didn't need this irresponsible beach bum telling her how to run her life, regardless of how hot and fast his touch made her blood race through her veins.

She refused to accept a nagging thought telling her it felt good to have someone want to take care of her, even if it wasn't necessary. She cast a wary eye at the ominous storm clouds before sliding open the door on the deck and stepping inside the house—the house she now officially shared with Blake for the summer.

He followed close on her heels. "Calm down." He grabbed her arm. "I'm not trying to run your life. You're free to do whatever you wish with whomever you wish."

She spun around, yanked her arm out of his grasp, and glared at him. "And don't you forget—"

The cat jumped out from behind a chair, bounded across the room at full speed, and leaped toward a startled Blake, landing on his shoulder.

"What the hell?"

Ty-Ling wrapped her paws gently around his neck, batted at his nose, flicked her tail across his face, then jumped back to the couch and to the floor. Before he could respond to the sudden flurry of activity, the cat wrapped its paws around his ankle, let go without digging its claws into his flesh, scampered away, and hid behind the couch.

Vicki didn't know what to do or say after Ty-Ling's hit and run. Then suddenly, she burst out laughing. She couldn't have stopped the laughter no matter how angry she had been just moments earlier. The shocked look on Blake's face and the cat's playful antics had done what his words had been unable to do. They'd penetrated her outer defense mechanism and gotten through to her reasonable inner person.

Blake let out a relieved chuckle. "Well, wonder of all wonders. That's the second time I've seen you laugh." His manner turned serious as he held her gaze with intensity. "You should do more of it, allow more spontaneous moments of fun into your life." He tenderly ran his fingertips lightly across her cheek. "It becomes you."

Tremors started deep inside her, followed by a shortness of breath. Her pulse raced. He'd done it to her again, pulled her into the mesmerizing control of his aura. Time seemed momentarily suspended. His lips brushed softly against her forehead. The next thing she knew, he had released her from his spell and disappeared upstairs. She stood in stunned silence for several seconds before regaining her composure. What had just happened, other than her once again obviously unacceptable behavior? She had no right to lash out at Blake. Had she alienated him with her angry words? What in the world had made her do such an odd thing?

She took a calming breath. The answer to that question was a frightening one, an answer she didn't want to even consider. An answer laden with layer upon layer of emotion. Vicki shook the objectionable thoughts from her mind and went into the dining room to finish unpacking boxes and arranging her office.

She still had several things to do before it would be properly organized for work the next morning.

****

Blake stood on the balcony outside his bedroom, unable to shake off his troubling thoughts. The wind had picked up considerably in the last hour. His nostrils flared as he inhaled the scent of approaching rain. Each physical encounter with Vicki, even the innocent brushing of his fingers against her skin, produced an increasingly emotional response inside him. As much as he wanted to bring her back to his bedroom for another sexual encounter intense enough to knock his socks off, he'd chosen the safer course of placing a light kiss on her forehead, then quickly retreating.

Retreating…hell, he'd flat out run away. Other than driving each other into a sexual frenzy, they had nothing in common. They existed in two different worlds. Why had he insisted she stay the summer? A truly foolish thing to have done. Too impetuous. Too impulsive.

And way too dangerous.

He closed his eyes and allowed the wind to ruffle his hair. Perhaps it could also ruffle thoughts of Vicki from his consciousness.

****

The first clap of thunder jarred Vicki from a restless sleep. The only sound breaking the quiet of the house came from the clock in the living room as it tolled midnight. The wind chimes on the deck made their own unique noise as the wind increased in intensity, indicating the storm's arrival. Raindrops spattered the windows, at first with just a trace of moisture, but quickly escalating into a full-blown downpour.

Rainstorms always made her uneasy, even without the fearful accompaniment of thunder and lightning. She pulled the covers tightly around her neck so that only her head peeked out from beneath them. Then her panic started. All the fear she'd experienced as a child in the Midwest welled inside her once again. A foolish, irrational fear, but that didn't stop it from being so.

Ty-Ling stationed herself in front of the bedroom door. Perhaps Vicki's trepidation over the impending storm had made her careless, but she had not closed the door enough for it to click shut. The cat nudged it open, entered the room, and jumped onto the bed. Vicki grabbed the cat, holding onto it like a security blanket.

"I'm glad to see you, Ty-Ling. I didn't want to be alone." She whispered the words, but the sound of her voice seemed very loud.

What she really wanted was to be safely wrapped in the security of Blake's arms. She fought the desire purely because of the emotional implications. She couldn't allow anything beyond a physical relationship with this man, nothing other than the incendiary desires and needs they shared. Nothing that could be construed as a portent for the future.

A flash of lightning filled the room with bright light before the loud clap of window-rattling thunder chased it away, the sound obliterating the noise of the howling wind and the rain pounding against the roof. Another bright flash and more thunder followed. Her entire body shivered. She held the cat tighter and buried her face in the pillow. She tried to control her sobs but couldn't stop the involuntary reaction.

She finally pulled the covers over her head and scrunched her body against the headboard as lightning momentarily lit up the room again. The mature, responsible woman had been enveloped by the fears of that little girl from long ago. Ty-Ling wiggled free of her tight grasp, jumped to the floor, and ran across the room and out her bedroom door as more thunder rumbled through the air. She heard the cat's yowl down the hall, the sound filling the air and competing with the thunder. Vicki cowered in fear beneath the covers, unable to move even to keep the cat from disturbing Blake.

Blake couldn't identify the noise, but that didn't stop it from jarring him out of a sound sleep. He lay in bed, his eyes closed, and tried to comprehend the weird sound. The noise continued, a shrill whining that penetrated above the sound of the storm.

The cat. He bolted upright, his senses jerking into full alert. He recognized the sound of the very upset Siamese, which seemed to come from the other side of his closed bedroom door. He threw back the covers and charged out of bed, a slight shiver darting across his skin as the cool air hit his body. He opened his door and stared down at the cat. It paced back and forth twitching its tail.

The cat did not try to attack his ankle. Instead, it started down the hall toward Vicki's room, stopped halfway, and turned back toward Blake. When he didn't follow, the cat returned and issued a plaintive cry. Then it started down the hall again. The cat was obviously trying to tell him something, but he didn't know what.

"Well, cat. What's on your mind? What's bothering you?"

Ty-Ling let out another plaintive cry and continued toward Vicki's door. Blake cautiously followed, not at all sure if he should. Vicki had been insistent on maintaining distance from him and once again, to his disappointment, retreated to her room shortly after dinner and stayed there the rest of the evening. He didn't understand why, but he had accepted her decision. He'd toyed with the notion that she had somehow felt pressured by him. Even though they were totally hot together, did she feel more obligation than desire? He wanted her in his bed, but only if she truly wanted to be there. The disturbing conflict continued to swirl through his mind even after he had gone to bed until he finally fell asleep.

As he approached the partially open door, he heard sobs coming from her room. He pushed it all the way open. The brief flash of lightning provided just enough illumination for him to see her huddled under the blanket. He rushed to her side.

"Vicki, are you okay?" He sat on the edge of the bed and pulled the cover off her head so he could see her face. The distress in her tear-filled eyes immediately tugged at the heart strings that had been winding around his senses since her unexpected arrival at his front door. The cat jumped on the bed and paced back and forth, emitting little cries as it paused to rub its head against her cheek.

"I—I'm fine."

"No, you're not. You're trembling." He gently wiped the tears from her cheeks. His logic told him he should leave her bedroom and allow her some distance because she'd made it clear that was what she wanted. His instincts, however, told him she needed comfort and reassurance. Or was his own need to hold her pushing at him?

He pulled her into his arms and held her close. Her firm breasts pressed against his chest, causing an involuntary shudder to ripple up his spine. A rush of excitement spread through his body, which he tried to ignore. She trembled as another bolt of lightning crackled across the sky.

"It's the storm, isn't it?" He kept his voice calm as he twined his fingers in her hair and gently rocked her in his arms.

"I'm all right. Honest." Her voice came out barely above a whisper. "Sorry you were disturbed. It's just this childish thing I have about thunder and lightning."

He liked holding her, liked the sensation of warmth and contentment—a strange feeling separate from wanting to drink in her essence and stroke his cock in and out of her hot pussy. Something he hadn't experienced in a very long time.

"Well, unless you have some strenuous objections," he pulled the blanket over them, "I'll stay here a little while longer. Just in case." He leaned against the headboard, more sitting than reclining, with her snuggled into his embrace. He closed his eyes, allowing the sounds of the storm to chase away the heated desire churning inside him, desire totally inappropriate to the situation.

It was not a time for steamy sex or to indulge the heated desire neither of them seemed able to resist. Even more surprising, he found the intimacy and closeness very satisfying as well as confusing. A slight frown wrinkled his forehead. He also found it a little frightening in its implications, a fear he didn't know how to handle.

****

Blake opened his eyes and looked around. Morning had arrived but without the sun. The rain had continued throughout the night without letting up, even though the thunder and lightning had passed. He had dozed rather than slept as he held Vicki in his arms. His back ached from maintaining an uncomfortable position against the headboard. He finally eased his arms from around her and slipped out of bed, careful not to wake her. As he headed for the bathroom, the cat woke, stretched, then curled up in the warm spot where Blake had been.

The hot shower sprayed across his back, soothing his muscles as he attempted to stretch out the kinks. They were both fully aware of their differing philosophies on life causing momentary conflicts. Even those *inconveniences* did not dampen their enthusiasm for indulging all the facets of heated sex. But last night was not one of those times. And last night had more of an impact on him than he wanted to admit. He had tried to fight off the thoughts and feelings tugging at his reality. Yet, holding Vicki had felt so right. This compulsively organized woman belonged in his arms, in his bed.

In his life.

He dried himself and dressed in a pair of faded jeans and a sweatshirt, the weather having turned decidedly cooler with the rainstorm. He paused at his bedroom door before walking to his dresser. Removing the photograph of his son from the box, he stared at it for several seconds. His grief and sorrow didn't seem quite as heavy as it had been. Maybe there was some hope for him after all. A future.

Closing his eyes, he tried to compose the turmoil, then placed the photo on the dresser. His thoughts remained a tangled web of confusion, all of them centering around Vicki. He took a moment to peek into her room. She appeared to still be asleep. He headed for the kitchen to make some coffee, leaving Ty-Ling on her bed.

The cat stretched and began to groom itself, licking its paws and rubbing them against its face. The activity stirred Vicki awake. She slowly opened her eyes, looking around as she sat up. Blake wasn't in the room. She recalled falling asleep in his arms but had not been aware of when he left. The bed still held his body heat.

As much as she craved the exquisite things his touch did to her body, the sexual rapture that raced through her veins every time they made love, there had been something so very right about the way he held her in his arms last night and comforted her fears. But this morning when she woke, she had experienced a moment of disappointment when she discovered he wasn't there. Making love first thing in the morning when they woke had become the most perfect way to start the day. And glancing around her empty bed told her how much she wished he had stayed until she woke up.

As she looked out the rain-streaked window, she allowed a little frown to crease her brow.

"At least the thunder and lightning have stopped." She shooed the cat from the bed. "Come on, Ty-Ling. It's time to get up."

She hurried into the bathroom to take her shower

and dress for the day. Her thoughts presented a combination of warm contentment at the memory of Blake's comforting embrace and a growing sense of apprehension and embarrassment at the prospect of facing him after her childish display of irrational fear. He had seen her vulnerability, glimpsed inside her carefully constructed façade of order and organization.

She finally made her way downstairs at eight-thirty, much later than normal for her. Blake had not been upstairs, and she didn't see him anywhere downstairs, although he had made coffee. Surely, he wouldn't be jogging in the pouring rain. What could be so important that he would have gone out in such terrible weather? She gave a little shrug and fixed Ty-Ling's breakfast.

After grabbing a mug of hot coffee, she headed toward the dining room to start her work day, already an hour behind schedule. She soon became totally absorbed in her work.

****

Blake drove into the garage and entered the house through the side door. It had been three hours since he left to run a few errands. He paused at the dining room door and watched Vicki work. A minute later, she looked up. Her startled expression said she hadn't heard him come home.

"I didn't want to disturb you." He offered her a friendly smile. "How are you feeling this morning? Any better?"

"A little foolish." A pink tinge came to her cheeks. He maintained eye contact with her. He wasn't asking an idle question just to be polite, wasn't judging her or ridiculing her fears. His concern was very real.

"I'm, uh, sorry you were bothered with my problem last night. It's just that, well, ever since I was a little girl, I've always been afraid of thunderstorms. I know it's silly, a totally irrational fear, but…" She dropped her gaze to the table as the crimson blush of embarrassment covered more than her cheeks. "That doesn't make it any less frightening for me."

"Everyone has their own private fears and personal demons." He reflected on the idea that perhaps his refusal to think about the future was rooted in his fear of how empty it seemed to be. "Well, I see you're busy. I won't keep you." He started to leave, then hesitated and turned back toward her, his voice less than confident. "Uh, while I was out this morning, I drove past the rental agency's office." He cleared his throat and nervously shifted his weight from one foot to the other.

The audible sigh that escaped her lips and the way her shoulders sagged in resignation said it all. "You don't need to tell me. Nobody was there, and the office was closed."

"I'm sorry." He left the dining room, stopping in the living room to build a fire in the fireplace, something bright and warm to combat the rainy day's gloom and the disappointment and hurt on her face. After he was satisfied with the fire, he picked up the package he'd dumped on the couch when he first came in from the garage.

Placing it on the kitchen table, he opened it much like a child did with a new toy. In fact, a *toy* was exactly what the package contained. He had bought a kite for Vicki, a stunt kite for beginners, just like the one he'd purchased for his son on the boy's sixth birthday. It was smaller than a regular stunt kite and constructed so it would disassemble rather than break if it crashed to the ground. As soon as the weather cleared, he would teach her to fly it. Maybe he could talk her into entering the summer competition in the adult beginner division.

He sat back for a moment, sipping his coffee. He visualized the excitement in her eyes when the box kite had soared into the sky. The memory of her laughter filled him with warmth. She needed more fun in her life, needed to get out from under her tightly controlled lifestyle. And he wasn't thinking about sex, either. She needed to laugh more. He stared at the brightly patterned red, orange, and yellow nylon fabric that made up the kite.

His mind turned to his growing connection to Vicki Templeton, a woman more of a paradox than anything else. One moment a totally uninhibited, hot, driving passion. The next moment, compulsively organized. And a moment later, almost painfully shy and easily embarrassed. All three facets of her personality tugged hard at his emotions.

Chapter Six

The rain continued through the middle of the week. Blake didn't tell Vicki about the kite he'd bought for her. He was sure she would label it a bunch of foolishness and insist he return it. He preferred to wait until the weather cleared when he could teach her to fly it. Their cohabitation seemed to have settled into a fairly comfortable day-to-day routine. They didn't interfere with each other's activities, but still found time to indulge their sexual desires on a regular basis, including what had become a daily ritual of morning sex before breakfast. And each time, the physical included an ever increasing emotional element, something he was not at all sure he wanted to openly acknowledge.

Though Vicki remained busy with her work during the day, Blake became restless being cooped up inside the house. He tried to convince himself it was only a temporary situation due to the rain, and each day he made a valiant effort to find something to do. But he always ended up spending more time staring out the rain-streaked sliding glass door than anything else. It was during those times his mind turned to the dangerous, unexplored territory of what the future held. And more often than not, those thoughts about the future included Vicki.

"Would you like to go to a movie?"

"What?" She looked up from her work, a startled expression on her face. "A movie? You mean, do I want to rent a video tonight?"

"No. I mean go out to a movie. The rain seems to have stopped, and the sky's beginning to clear. We can catch the early matinee at the village theater."

The frown that immediately creased her brow told him she disapproved of his suggestion. She rearranged some of the papers on the dining room table, the slight tug of irritation pulling at her sense of what made up appropriate and responsible behavior clearly visible to him. "I couldn't possibly take off in the middle of a weekday just to go to a movie. I have work to do."

"You're self-employed and work at home, so what difference does it make if you do the work on a weekday or a weekend, during the day, or in the evening? We can either go now or later this afternoon." A blanket of determination settled over him. One way or another, he intended to see that she allowed some time in her day for fun and recreation. He walked around behind her, pulled the chair away from the table with her still sitting in it, then grabbed her hand and hauled her to her feet.

"Come on. It's a comedy. It won't hurt you to take a two hour break and have some laughs. Think of it as a long lunch hour." A teasing grin played at the corners of his mouth. "You can make it up by staying in your office an hour later tonight."

"I said no." She tugged her hand free of his grasp. "I have work to do. Perhaps another time. I could check my schedule to see when—"

"Ah, yes." He couldn't keep the sarcasm out of his voice. "That carefully planned schedule that accounts for every minute of your life. It seems you leave me no options. You won't go to the movies with me, so I guess I'll have to find something else for us to do right here...*right now.*"

Before she had an opportunity to protest, he glanced at his watch, then quickly made a notation on her daily planner. He placed his hands on her shoulders, plumbed the depths of her eyes for a moment, and flashed a truly mischievous grin as he pointed to the calendar.

"You don't have any choice. It's on your schedule."

Before she could react, he cupped her face and captured her mouth with a soft kiss. He pulled back, then quickly brushed his lips against hers again. He grabbed the pen and made another entry on her daily planner. A satisfied little grin tugged at his lips. One way or another, he intended to loosen up her tightly controlled existence and teach her how to have fun. Perhaps he, too, could learn to truly enjoy life again rather than just going through the motions. He turned and left the room.

Vicki watched Blake climb the stairs. Several seconds passed before she collected her senses and composed the tremors of excitement dancing inside her. She glanced at her schedule book. In large, bold letters, next to the appropriate time slot, he had printed *kiss Blake.* Beneath that notation, in the next fifteen minute time slot, he'd written *play game of stable boy ravishes innocent milk maiden* and had drawn a line to block out the next two hours.

A smile slowly curled her lips. Even though they had indulged their sexual appetite first thing that morning, a rush of moisture dampened her panties and her nipples puckered into taut buds. How was it possible for him to turn her neatly ordered existence into a mass of disorganized confusion? For the first time in her life, she made the decision to abandon her work in the middle of a weekday for the sole purpose of pandering to her own pleasure. And what was worse, she knew she wanted more of him—so much more.

Ty-Ling interrupted her thoughts by jumping onto the table and making herself comfortable in the middle of Vicki's paperwork. She stroked the cat's fur, then picked up the animal. "Oh, Ty-Ling. What have I gotten myself into? He's not at all the type of man I want, yet he makes my insides quiver like an impressionable school girl. I can't think straight when he touches me. All my good intentions simply sail away on the breeze…" She furrowed her brow. "Just like that kite did."

Vicki set the cat on the floor. Her breath came a little faster, her heart beat a little harder, and her entire body tingled in anticipation.

She made a quick trip through the kitchen to get a glass of milk and carried it upstairs, but found Blake's bedroom empty. She continued on down the hall to her room, pausing at the door when she saw his nude body stretched out on her bed. A little grin tugged at her lips. Of course. For the concept of the game, it made sense that he would lie in wait for her in her room rather than assuming an innocent milk maiden would actually go to the stable boy's room. An unaccustomed moment of frivolous fun assailed her as she entered her bedroom.

"Oh, my goodness. It's such a warm day, and this milk is getting so very heavy. I think I'll set it down and rest for a bit before continuing back to the house, perhaps remove some of this heavy clothing and take advantage of the slight breeze. After all, there's no one here. I'm sure I'll be perfectly safe from prying eyes…and other unwanted attentions."

She placed the glass on the nightstand next to Blake, then unbuttoned her shirt. She raked her gaze over the length of his nude body, taking particular delight in the sight of his marvelous erection and knowing the delicious treat would soon belong to her in any number of exciting ways. She noted the twinkle in his eyes as he watched her play out the role he had assigned her. A strange sensation engulfed her—the thrill of exhibitionism she had never before experienced. Just knowing he watched as she portrayed the innocent milk maiden added a new thrill to her already stimulated body.

She removed her clothes, then pretended to fan herself as she sat on the edge of the bed. "Ah, that's much better. The cool breeze is so soothing on my bare skin."

Blake snaked his arms around her waist from behind and held her in place. His hot breath tickled across her ear.

"Well, well, well…what have we here?" He cupped her breasts and pulled her back against his chest. "I think it's time for my innocent little milk maiden to learn the way of the world."

"No…please don't." His touch made it difficult for her to continue playing the part, the thought of saying no in direct opposition to the need throbbing in her pussy. She wanted to impale herself on his rigid shaft, to feel him deep inside her as he shuttled in and out.

"Just relax, my pretty one. You'll like what I'm going to do to you."

"No, you can't do this." She squirmed in his arms, as if trying to free herself, but the movement only reinforced the need throbbing between her legs. "I'll be forever ostracized, considered damaged goods."

"Not if you don't tell anyone." He nibbled at her earlobe and kneaded the firm flesh of her breasts. Her insides quivered with desire. "It will be our little secret." The stable boy shoved her onto her back in the softness of the bed and quickly straddled her legs. He leered at her, a look filled with a raw sexuality that had her pussy close to clenching in orgasmic contractions without even being touched. "A secret we can share again and again."

"No, you must not. I'm begging you." She forced out the words, the quaver in her voice very real but not from fear. "The master of the house, he won't…"

"So, my innocent little milk maiden isn't so innocent after all. The master has been fucking you?" A glow of excitement flashed in Blake's eyes. "That means I won't need to be so gentle after all. Your cherry has already been plucked. You know the feel of a cock. In that case, I intend to make you scream in delight and beg me to fuck you again and again. You'll forget all about the master once I've introduced you to what a real man has to offer. The lady of the house can give testimony as to my prowess. She refers to the master as *that barely adequate little prick*."

"No." Vicki had never played a fantasy game before, but Blake obviously had, and he was good at it. It was all she could do to remain still and feign fear. He had not fingered her pussy or as much as touched her clit, obviously knowing full well how she craved his expert seduction. "The master will be harsh with me if he thinks—"

"He won't know unless you tell him." His mouth came down hard on hers, totally dominating her existence. His kiss demanded everything of her. His lips were soft and pliant, yet controlling the very breath that filled her lungs. He thrust his tongue into her mouth, aggressively seeking and tasting every hidden corner.

To hell with the game. She didn't want to play, didn't want to pretend to put him off. She was ready to scream out her desires and needs, to beg him to fuck her long and hard until neither of them had the energy to move. Until her pussy radiated enough heat to raise the temperature in the room and set off the sprinkler system.

Blake took the decision out of her hands.

His chest heaved with his labored breathing. His cock pulsed with need, but not just for the mindless activity of getting off. The need was specifically for Vicki. He was done with the game. He had to have her right now. Flailing toward the nightstand, he sought one of the condom packets he'd placed there. He accidently knocked over the glass of milk spilling it on the floor but didn't care. With trembling hands, he expertly sheathed his erection.

Once again, he captured her mouth with a kiss that clearly conveyed all the passion coursing through his veins. Their tongues twined in a dance of seduction, the textures meshing together. Using his knee, he nudged her legs wider apart and settled himself between them. He wanted to immediately plunge his throbbing dick inside her, but held off long enough to make sure she was ready. He slipped his finger between her pussy lips into the moist heat of her body. The quick jerk of her hips against his hand pleased him. He added a second finger, drawing them in and out of her wet slit as he stimulated her clit with his thumb.

Vicki's insides contracted in orgasmic rapture. Her pussy muscles grabbed at his fingers. His kiss, his touch. It didn't take much for him to send her over the edge into euphoria. Just being in the same room with him started her juices flowing. The sudden loss when he withdrew his fingers lasted only a second. His cockhead probed her opening, then he slid his shaft into her still convulsing tunnel. She wrapped her legs around his hips, her arms around his neck, and held on for the incredible ride.

His confident strokes kept her in a heightened state of orgasmic frenzy. They grew harder and shorter, until he pumped on the edge of his own release. Two more deep thrusts, and his body shuddered. He held her until the spasms subsided.

And then he continued to hold her.

Neither of them made even the slightest attempt to untangle their entwined bodies, their contentment whole and all consuming. Vicki allowed a brief thought about needing to get back to work but told herself the two hours marked off in her daily planner weren't up yet. A hint of a smile pulled at her lips. As recently as a couple of days ago, she would have been shocked by that decision. But now, she didn't give a damn about the work waiting downstairs.

"Let's buy some chocolate body paint and whipped cream." His words tickled across her ear. "And maybe some other toys, too."

Other than her own vibrator used in privacy when she was horny and alone, she had never played with sex toys, and certainly not with someone else, in spite of her one-time attempt at a *ménage a trois*. A little shiver of excitement fluttered inside her as her anticipation grew. The thought of licking chocolate off Blake's delicious dick tantalized her. And the whipped cream…they could do any number of things with that.

"What kind of *other toys* do you have in mind?" She nipped at his shoulder blade with her lips, then licked his nipples. His skin tasted so good. Everything about him tasted good. And she wanted more.

"I'll let it be a surprise. And I promise you won't be disappointed."

"Mmm, nothing you've done so far has been disappointing."

Blake wanted her again. He wanted her now. He slid out of bed, disposed of the used condom, and grabbed a new one. Hunger gnawed at him, a deep need he wasn't sure would ever be completely filled. No matter how many times he had Vicki, no matter how great the sex, he still didn't have enough of her. He had never felt so much at one with another woman. Had never felt as close to anyone other than his immediate family. His mother, his father…and his son.

He lifted her legs over his shoulders, cupped her ass cheeks in his hands, and raised her hips off the bed. And with one swift thrust, he plunged deep inside her, filling her tunnel with his hard shaft. He remained still and reveled in the way her pussy walls closed around his shaft. Then he started long sure strokes, each one burying his dick deeper inside her. He shuttled in and out with ever increasing intensity, thrusting harder and faster. The sight of her boobs jiggling and bouncing with each thrust added to his excitement.

Her orgasmic contractions squeezed his cock, pulling it farther in until it felt as if his balls might be sucked into her pussy. Hard spasms of orgasm shuddered through him, and every nerve ending in his body erupted in exquisite rapture. His chest heaved as he tried to gulp in enough air. He eased her legs off his shoulders, then quickly turned over onto his back with her on top of him—his cock still buried deep, her convulsing pussy holding on to it.

He squeezed and kneaded the firm flesh of her ass cheeks, pausing every few seconds to run his fingers along her crevice and stimulate her anus. She didn't pull away from his touch, something that pleased him. He thoroughly enjoyed all facets of sex play but didn't want to push her into participation where she felt uncomfortable. Hopefully, this was something they could further explore in the very near future. Maybe she'd be into that at some point. He hoped so.

****

"That's one of the funniest films I've seen in a long time." Vicki's exuberance flowed with the same excitement as her words. She continued to laugh over a particularly funny scene from the movie as they emerged from the theater.

Blake put his arm around her shoulders and drew her closer. "I really like seeing you laugh. Your whole face lights up. You should relax more often, let your hair down, have fun."

She shot him a sly look. "You mean fun other than what should only be enjoyed behind closed doors? Unless you're into really kinky stuff."

"Oh? Are you saying if I took you outside on the deck, bent you over the railing, and had my way with you, that would be kinky? But if I bent you over the kitchen table and had my way with you behind closed doors, then it wouldn't?" He looked at her questioningly, a teasing grin playing across his lips.

Heated embarrassment flushed her cheeks. Her actions had surprised her when she agreed to go to the movie with him rather than returning to work after their *scheduled* time out for a sex romp.

He gave her shoulder an extra little squeeze before they started down the street. "Uh oh." He glanced up at the angry sky. "Maybe we shouldn't have walked to the theater. Looks like it's going to rain again. We'd better hurry home rather than stopping to get something to eat."

"I think you're right." The light-hearted fun of the movie and the protection of his arm around her felt good. *We'd better hurry home*. His words about them going home suffused her with a tender warmth, almost a feeling of longing for what might be possible with this completely wrong man. The words carried the sound and feel of permanency, the same type of permanency and security she'd been determined to provide for herself. As if she and Blake actually belonged together.

No. She had to stop those thoughts before they progressed any further. Regardless of how he made her feel, it didn't change the fact that he didn't have a job and seemed to have no desire or ambition toward finding gainful employment. The question darted through her mind again about how he could afford to lease the beach house. Where did he get his money to pay his bills? Maybe an inheritance of some type. She dismissed her concern, trying to convince herself his finances were none of her business.

They walked briskly down the street toward the beach house but only made it half a block before it started to sprinkle. They quickened their pace. The sprinkle soon turned into a shower, forcing them to run the remaining block to the house. Blake and Vicki burst through the front door, each of them laughing in spite of being wet.

"I'm soaked." Vicki set her purse on the table and tousled her fingers through her wet hair, pushing the matted strands away from her face. "It's a good thing it was only a shower rather than the rain we had earlier this week."

"I'll put some logs in the fireplace and build a fire. You should probably get out of those wet clothes so you don't catch a cold."

She gave him a sly grin. "Out of my wet clothes and into your dry bed?"

"Tell me, Victoria Templeton, who are you?" He pulled her into his arms. His voice turned soft. "Or maybe the question should be, *what* are you? An unbelievably sexy seductress sent to mesmerize and enslave every man whose path you cross? An ultra-organized woman so concerned about tomorrow she won't allow any time in her life to enjoy today? Or an almost painfully shy woman who isn't sure about herself, about where and how she fits in? I can't figure out which one is the real you." He placed a tender kiss on her forehead. "Or are you all of them rolled into one incredibly enticing woman?"

She closed her eyes and tried to collect some kind of logic. "I thought I knew exactly who I was, what I wanted out of life, and how I was going to get it." Uncertainty coursed through her veins. "Then I ran into you. Now I can't make heads or tails of anything. Every time I try to get my life back on my planned course, you pull me into some sort of weird parallel universe where nothing is the way I thought it should be. I just don't know anymore."

She slipped her arms around his waist. They stood together for the longest time. Neither of them saying anything. Neither of them making any effort to move. Neither of them wanting to break the spell binding them together. Disturbing and unsettling thoughts circulated through her mind. He totally muddled her usually clear thinking process, turning her need for logic and consistency into a shambles.

"Know what I'd like to do?" His words brushed softly across her cheek.

A wry grin tugged at the corners of her mouth. "Hmm, I wonder how many guesses that will take me."

"If it's more than one, then you need to take your crystal ball in for repairs." A slight frown wrinkled his forehead. "Mmm, I don't know if it's a good thing for you to be able to read my mind like that."

****

The morning sun shone brightly in defiance of the forecast of more rain by early afternoon. After making coffee, Blake took out the beginner's stunt kite he'd purchased for Vicki. It was a perfect morning for kite flying. A sudden thought occurred to him. He glanced toward the stairs and listened. When he heard the shower, he knew it would be a little while before she appeared downstairs. He went into the dining room, then returned to the kitchen a minute later.

He looked around for anything that might pull her attention, anything she could claim as something she needed to do right away. His gaze lit on the furry little beast. He put out food and fresh water for Ty-Ling and even cleaned the cat box. Other than eating breakfast if she wanted some, nothing else should draw Vicki's attention away from his plans.

"Good morning." She walked directly to the coffee maker. "Fresh coffee...smells good."

He poured her a mug and set it on the table next to his. "What would you like to have for breakfast? I'm cooking."

An amused chuckle escaped her throat. "Why do I feel like I'm being rushed?" She glanced around, then shot him a questioning look. "What's going on?"

"Going on? What makes you think that? It's a beautiful morning. I thought we might take a walk on the beach before you go to work."

"That's it? Then why do you look like you're hiding something? Are you going to tell me?" A knowing grin turned up the corners of her mouth. She snuggled her body next to his and lowered her voice to a seductive whisper as she slowly unzipped his shorts. "Or do I need to resort to drastic measures to get the information out of you?"

"Mmm..." He thrust his hips forward and ground his cock against her hand. "I was about to make a full confession, but I think I'll hold out and let you have your way with me until I break under the pressure."

"Tell me." She withdrew her hand and playfully swatted his chest. "What's on your mind, other than the obvious?"

He made an exaggerated effort of composing

himself. "I bought you a present the other day, and I've been waiting for a sunny morning to give it to you."

"A present?" Confusion wrinkled her brow. "For me?"

"Yep. And as soon as we finish breakfast, I'll show it to you."

Vicki wasn't sure what to think or how to respond. He bought something for her? A present? Why would he do that? Suddenly, it all felt way too personal. They had been fully indulging their sexual desires, sometimes two and three times a day. That certainly qualified as personal. So why did his buying her a present suddenly seem so much more personal than sex?

"I thought I'd just take some juice and maybe a carton of yogurt into my office and have it while I'm working. You've sort of gotten me off schedule." A rush of desire accompanied by dampness seeping across the crotch of her panties confirmed exactly why she'd gotten off schedule.

"Just juice and yogurt? Maybe you should check your daily planner and see if that's on your schedule for this morning."

She furrowed her brow, once more confused, then recalled the *stable boy and the innocent milk maiden* notation he'd put on her calendar yesterday. She rushed out of the kitchen and into the dining room. Grabbing her planner, she looked at the time slots for that morning. He had blocked out the time from eight o'clock until ten with the words *kite flying lessons*. He'd even drawn a small picture of a kite.

She turned to find him standing in the doorway holding a small kite. She wasn't sure what to say or how to respond. "I...I can't."

"Yes, you can. The forecast is for rain again this afternoon. You can work then. But this morning is bright and sunny, and the breeze is perfect. This is a beginner's stunt kite. I'll teach you how to fly it."

The memory of her one and only attempt at flying a kite filled her mind—the embarrassment of falling down and losing the kite. That memory, however, became tempered by the thrill she'd experienced as it lifted higher and higher into the air, the strong tug of the kite string against her hand, the bright colors soaring into the sky. Then a thud of harsh reality hit her. A week ago, she wouldn't have given such a silly waste of time a moment's thought. Now, she was about to agree. She glanced at the next page and noticed that he'd added Tim's party on the schedule for Saturday night.

The twinkle in his eyes and the smug expression on his face said more than words. She tilted her head to one side and raised an eyebrow. "You seem quite pleased with yourself. Is this now an established, ongoing thing with you? I'll need to constantly check my schedule to see what you think I should be doing?"

"Well, I hadn't thought of it in those exact terms, but it sounds like a good idea to me." He flashed her one of his dazzling smiles that never failed to soften her. As much as she wanted to be stern and businesslike, she couldn't keep a grin from lifting the corners of her mouth. "Looks like I'm going to have to lock up my daily planner if I intend to get any work done."

"Come on. Let's go fly a kite." He grabbed her hand. "I promise to let you go to work at ten o'clock, and you can stay in your office for the rest of the day.

Until five o'clock, if you want. Tomorrow's Saturday. Even by your own definition, it's a non-work day. And Tim's party is tomorrow night, just like it says on your schedule."

"Since tomorrow's a non-work day, why can't we fly the kite then?"

"Because, my delicious temptation, right now it's sunny. This afternoon and tomorrow are supposed to be rainy." A mischievous grin pulled at the corners of his mouth. "You plan to work this afternoon, but for tomorrow we'll need to find some sort of indoor activity to occupy our time before the party. I'm open to ideas, especially lewd and kinky ones."

Vicki couldn't hold back a laugh. She shook her head in resignation. "How can I possibly argue with such solid logic?"

"You can't." He led her outside onto the deck, where he showed her how to assemble the kite. After he explained the differences between a stunt kite and a box kite, they ventured onto the beach.

The soft sand felt good squishing between her toes. The sound of the seagulls and the waves breaking on shore filled her with a sense of contentment and well-being. How marvelous it would be to live here all the time. How carefree—

Her thoughts came crashing down around her. How ideal it sounded to be able to enjoy the beach every day, to sit on the deck and bask in a glorious sunset. To fall asleep every night in Blake Callahan's arms after making love. To awaken every morning and start the day by making love again. Ideal, yes.

But practical? Realistic? Not even close.

Blake handed her the kite. "Okay, remember what I

told you? Are you ready?"

"As ready as I'll ever be." She took in a steadying breath. "Hopefully, I won't lose this one."

"If it decides to fly away, then that's the way it is." He gave her hand an intimate little squeeze and flashed her a confident smile. "No harm done."

She followed his instructions and soon, with his encouragement, had the kite flying high in the air. Her exhilaration soared, making her feel almost as high as the colorful kite. He guided her through a few basic stunt maneuvers until she was able to perform them on her own. For two hours they stayed out on the sand laughing, playing, and enjoying the moment. It had been a long time since she had felt so unencumbered. The freeing sensation lifted her spirits higher than they'd been in years. Maybe higher than they had ever been. She even admitted she might have been just a little bit too preoccupied with planning for the future, that her life wasn't as well rounded and balanced as it might be.

And that realization left her unsettled and confused. All her carefully held notions and beliefs weren't holding up against the onslaught of Blake Callahan's mesmerizing presence.

The clock registered nearly eleven-thirty before Vicki finally returned to her office to start her work day, an hour and a half later than the ten o'clock notation written on her schedule. Where had the time gone? No, she didn't need to ask herself that question. She already knew the answer. She had lost all track of time because she was…well, she was having fun. No more, no less. She had been simply enjoying herself for a carefree morning at the beach.

She remained in her office the rest of the afternoon, working steadily to make up for the time she'd spent that morning playing hooky. As Blake had predicted, the afternoon turned cloudy, then dark, and the rain finally returned about four-thirty with no signs of letting up any time soon. By five o'clock, she decided to call it a day. The smell of burning wood in the fireplace attracted her attention. She wandered into the living room, where she found Blake stretched out on the couch reading a book.

He looked up when she entered the room. "Are you through for the day?"

"Yes." She allowed a moment of consideration before admitting to her decision. "In fact, I'm through in my office for the weekend."

She had difficulty making the decision, especially after taking the morning off to play on the beach. It went against everything she'd thought she held near and dear.

He inserted a bookmark, then closed the book and set it on the end table. Holding out his hand, he beckoned her to join him. He sat up and scooted over to make room. "Well, that's quite an admission, coming from you. What brought this on?"

She sat next to him. The sensual pull of his animal magnetism immediately grabbed her. The overwhelming power of his mere presence, of the slightest touch of his skin, sent waves of desire crashing through her. She had been preoccupied with sex from the moment she'd first seen him. But was that really a bad thing? If two people were physically compatible and enjoyed the pleasures of sex, then why should it be considered wrong? Why should they deny themselves?

Not that she'd been denying herself where Blake was concerned.

He slid his hand beneath her shirt and cupped her bare breast. She closed her eyes and emitted a soft moan of delight. His touch had become as natural as night following day. Would the intensely heated passion they shared eventually cool? Was hot sex their only common ground? He held her in his arms, brushed a tender kiss across her lips, then cradled her head against his shoulder.

The rain continued. Large droplets hitting the sliding glass door joined the crackle of the fire, creating a sensual harmony that fed into the emotion-filled atmosphere surrounding them. But what to do about it?

Chapter Seven

Vicki and Blake finished dinner, then took their wine glasses into the living room so they could enjoy the last remnants of the fire. He jabbed at the remains of the smoldering logs with the fireplace poker, moving them around until flames flared again. Then he added another log and turned on some soft music. Leaning back into the corner of the sofa, he pulled her next to him. They each sipped their wine, enjoying the fire and simply being together.

He had never in his life felt as comfortable with another woman as he did with Vicki. Hot sex aside, just being with her filled him with the type of contentment he'd never known. The realization had been difficult for him to admit, even to himself. The last thing he'd been looking for was any type of relationship. It had not even been a consideration for him.

Yet, with Vicki, what had started as a fleeting notion had turned into a fully formed thought that continued to circulate through his mind. It felt so good having her in his arms. It all felt so right. Did he dare consider a future with her? A *real* future? The troubling thought continued to swirl around in his consciousness. Was he already too involved? In over his head?

He didn't know and seeking the answers frightened him.

He placed a tender kiss on her forehead. "Tell me,

my sexy beauty, what made you decide to take off from work for the entire weekend? It's certainly a different tune from the one you've been singing since you arrived at my door one week ago this afternoon."

"Only a week?" She blurted out the words, the realization clearly taking her by surprise. Then her voice took on a faraway sound, as if she were thinking out loud rather than talking to him. "It seems like it's been so much longer."

"Oh?" He tried without success to eliminate the teasing quality from his voice. "You mean the time's been dragging by so slowly it seemed like it surely must have been much longer than a week?"

A chuckle, half amused and half embarrassed, escaped her throat. "That's not at all what I meant." She twisted around to face him. With a slightly trembling finger, she traced the edge of his lower lip. Her tone softened until almost inaudible, but there was no mistaking the emotion that seeped through. "It's only been a week, but in that time you've managed to make a shambles out of my carefully ordered life." She placed a soft kiss on his lips. "I feel like I've known you forever."

Vicki closed her eyes and rested her head on his shoulder. He wrapped his arms around her and held her close.

"A lifetime, indeed." His whispered words tickled her ear. "I know exactly what you mean."

Neither of them spoke for a long time. The flames died down and then went out, plunging the room into near darkness. Only the light from the kitchen provided modest illumination.

Blake stirred first, finally rising from the sofa and

offering Vicki his hand. Neither of them spoke as he led her upstairs to his bedroom. The soft warmth of emotion continued to surround them. Their clothing fell away, and they nestled into the softness of his bed. He captured her mouth with a tender kiss, their deeply felt emotional connection replacing the frenzied need of hot sex.

He stroked her skin, its smooth, creamy texture sending a ripple of anticipation through him. But the anticipation presented itself as a loving closeness rather than a frantic need. He teased her nipple with his tongue before gently sucking first one breast, and then the other. The sensation of her fingers skimming lightly across his back and shoulders fed into his arousal. A sensual aura surrounded them as they made love, tenderly, gently, and with great care.

They remained wrapped in each other's arms, basking in the afterglow of their lovemaking until they finally drifted into a blissful sleep.

Saturday morning dawned bright and sunny, but with the forecast predicting more rain by noon. Blake had a quick errand to run, telling Vicki he would be right back. True to his word, he returned in twenty minutes with a surprise.

"It's a shame to waste this beautiful morning." Genuine enthusiasm filled his voice. "Especially with rain on its way again."

"I've never ridden one of these." Vicki stared at the bicycle-built-for-two. When Blake left to run his errand, she had no idea he intended to rent this contraption for the morning. "Is it much different than riding a regular bike?"

"A little, but not much. I'll sit in front, and you can

sit behind. The main thing for you to keep in mind is not to try and steer. Your handlebars are only something to hold on to, they don't move." He flashed her a teasing grin. "But that doesn't mean you can just sit back and let me do all the work. You do have to pedal, too."

"Well…" A quick jab of uncertainty had her biting her lip. She'd managed to conquer kite flying, so she shouldn't be concerned about this. After all, she knew how to ride a bicycle. Could a bicycle-built-for-two really be that different?

"Come on. We'll walk the bike over to the bike path, then ride to the pier and back."

"Sure." She allowed a warm smile to spread across her face. "That sounds like fun." *Fun.* Before meeting Blake, she hadn't used that word in a very long time. But somehow he'd made it an acceptable concept. She wasn't doing anything wrong taking time out to simply have fun. It didn't mean she'd be neglecting her work or the needs of her clients. It would get done on time, but meanwhile a little fun certainly wouldn't do any harm. "Besides, the exercise will be good for us."

"Oh? Haven't you been getting enough exercise lately? Perhaps I could help you remedy that." He winked at her as he tried to maintain a serious expression that quickly turned into a lewd grin. "I know an effective version of calisthenics we could try rather than going biking, something good for the cardio vascular system."

"Perhaps we could do both?" She returned his grin. "Ride the bicycle while the sun is shining and leave your excellent suggestion to this afternoon when the rain keeps us indoors?"

"A superb idea." He leaned his face into hers and placed a tender kiss on her lips.

They walked the dual bike to the riding path. It took Vicki a couple of tries to get the hang of riding it, then they were on their way down the beach to the pier. The ocean breeze ruffled her hair. The clean air filled her lungs. It had been a long time since she'd felt as alive as she had the last few days. A long time since she'd indulged in frivolous activities for no reason other than the pure enjoyment of having a good time. And Blake was the one responsible. He had cajoled, pushed, and practically dragged her screaming into the arena of fun. Kite flying. A bicycle-built-for-two. Activities she never would have believed she'd be doing. And she was so very thankful he had persisted in his efforts.

Rather than starting back when they had covered the short distance to the pier, they pedaled on for another mile before turning around. On the way home, they stopped at the pier for a snack and a cold drink before continuing their ride. They found a table on the café's patio, where they enjoyed the sun while keeping an eye on the approaching storm clouds.

Blake covered Vicki's hand with his. Maintaining physical contact with her, no matter how fleeting or minimal, filled him with a settled feeling of contentment unlike anything he had ever known. They enjoyed their leisurely rest stop, talking quietly and basking in the momentary warmth of the sun. Before long, the sun disappeared behind the storm clouds and a cool breeze picked up. They rode back to the house and arrived just in time to keep from getting wet. Blake made a quick trip to return the bicycle to the rental shop.

While waiting for Blake to come back, Vicki wandered onto the covered deck to watch the rain. As long as there wasn't any thunder and lightning involved, she liked the gentle patter of the raindrops. Her thoughts turned to Tim's party scheduled for later that night. She hadn't told Blake, but she had mixed feelings about it. She'd taken an instant dislike to Tim when they had met with him to discuss her bogus rental agreement and getting her money back. True to his word, he had written Mr. Edwards and provided her with a copy of his letter. Unfortunately, the rental agent had not responded.

A sigh of resignation told her she'd known all along there wouldn't be a reply. Between Gary Sanderson's comment about taking the house away from the rental agency and now getting no response to the letter from an attorney, she admitted she needed to file a police report. She would do that first thing Monday.

Something about Tim had set her nerves on edge, and not in a good way. She tried to adopt a more philosophical attitude. After all, it was just a party. A lot of people would be there. No reason for Tim to make any more unwanted advances toward her. But the idea of going inside his house again still left her uneasy.

Then the image of the blonde rubbing against Blake after the volleyball game popped into her mind. Would she be at the party, too? What about other women Blake had slept with? Vicki shook her head to clear it of the intrusive thoughts. Blake's past was none of her business, just like any of her previous sex partners were none of his, at least, not as a negative thought that could justify jealousy.

Jealousy. The word hit her like a ton of bricks. She had no right to be jealous, especially based on nothing more than stray thoughts. But the realization told her something far more disturbing. It screamed out her emotional involvement with Blake Callahan, a man unsuited to what she wanted out of life.

But exactly what did she want? Confusion swirled through her mind. So much had happened during the last week, things she'd never imagined could be real. Was Blake a better fit for her life than she had at first wanted to believe?

Vicki jumped in surprise when Blake snaked his arms around her waist and pressed his lips against the side of her neck. "I'll give you two choices. We can either take a walk in the rain or go upstairs and see if we can find some worthwhile way to pass the time on this rainy afternoon."

"Only two choices?" she teased.

"Actually, there's only one viable choice I can think of. How about you?"

She turned in his arms until she faced him while trying to suppress a sly grin. She slipped her arms around his neck. "It's a tough decision, so I'll leave it up to you." She feigned a look of innocence as she tilted her head to one side and batted her eyelashes. "What do you think we should do?"

He slid his hands down her back, cupped her bottom, and pulled her hips against his as he nibbled her earlobe. "Follow me, and I'll show you."

She thrust her pelvis forward and rubbed seductively against his growing erection. "Aren't you going to give me even a little bit of a hint?"

Taking her hand in his, Blake led the way upstairs

to his bedroom. Without even a pretense at hesitation, they dropped their clothes to the floor and fell into his bed. She wrapped her leg around his thigh, opening herself to his tantalizing touch. He slowly inserted his finger between her pussy lips and stimulated her already engorged clit with his thumb. Her soft moans and look of delight fed his obvious arousal. He had never known anyone more responsive than Vicki. Their body chemistry meshed perfectly. They had been totally in sync with each other's needs and wants from that first night.

He increased his manipulation of her clit and added a second finger inside her slick pussy. In no time at all, she succumbed to the first of what he hoped would be many orgasms. He had never received so much pleasure from satisfying a woman as he did with her. He thrilled to the way she totally abandoned herself to sensation, to the exquisite look of satisfaction that covered her face when in the throes of an orgasm. So genuine. So real. So exciting.

So *perfect.*

With a quick move, he slid down her body and teased her clit with his tongue before sucking it into his mouth. In only a second, her soft moans of delight turned to cries of orgasmic bliss and her convulsions claimed her. The intense sensation raced directly to Blake's cock.

In a highly efficient and smooth maneuver, he positioned her on her stomach with her legs drawn up and spread to each side. After rolling on a condom, he rested his chest against her back and wrapped his arms around her hips. His cock head probed between her pussy lips from behind, then he thrust into her wet tunnel until his shaft was buried all the way to his balls. A groan of pure ecstasy clawed its way out of his throat, enhanced by the way she shoved back and wiggled her ass against his abdomen.

He played his fingers across her clit, alternately rubbing and plucking it to make sure she remained in a state of heightened stimulation. Her moans of pleasure grew louder. Her muscles clenched and contracted around his shaft, rhythmically milking him of his control as the contractions claimed her in another orgasm. He pumped into her with short, hard strokes until spasms of release shuddered through his body. His lungs fought for oxygen. His entire body rippled with the intensity of his release.

****

Blake and Vicki entered Tim's house through the sliding doors on the deck. The party was already in full swing. Tim immediately came over to them, shaking Blake's hand and kissing Vicki on the cheek. Was it her imagination, or had his lips lingered longer than necessary? Should she have said something to Blake about feeling uncomfortable around Tim? She tried to dismiss her concerns as inappropriate, just her imagination.

"I'm glad to see both of you." Tim bubbled with enthusiasm. "I was beginning to be concerned. I really thought with you living right next door, you'd be the first to arrive. But I guess you had *other* things to do?"

His lascivious grin and the way he eyed Vicki left her with no doubt about what he meant. A cold shiver told her she didn't want to be in his house. But in all fairness, could she expect Blake to leave the party just because she didn't want to be there? Would it have been appropriate to suggest he attend by himself? Tim had made a point of specifically inviting her rather than merely including her as part of Blake's invitation. And after all, Tim had written the letter to Mr. Edwards on her behalf. Would it have been rude to refuse his invitation?

She dismissed her concerns as being irrelevant. Besides, it was too late. They were at the party and needed to stay a polite amount of time. She certainly didn't want to cause Blake any embarrassment in front of his friend.

Tim grabbed her hand and pulled her out onto the dance floor. A fast song spilled out through the sound system, so dancing didn't really involve much touching. But no sooner had that thought pushed through her mind than a slow song began. Tim pulled her into his arms and moved to the music, holding her much tighter than she wanted. She looked around, trying to spot Blake, to signal him for help in gracefully extricating her from the awkward situation. But to her dismay, he had his back to her and seemed to be engaged in serious conversation with a man she didn't know

Then Tim rubbed his growing arousal against her stomach. "Let me take you on a tour of my house. We can start upstairs."

She tried to gracefully pull away, finally extracting herself from his arms. "I'm parched. I think I'll get myself something to drink."

"Allow me, my pretty one."

"Oh, please, don't go to the trouble." Something about the way he'd said that, the knowing look in his eyes, sent waves of caution crashing through her, and she felt the inexplicable need to make sure nothing would be slipped into her drink. She forced a smile. "You have a lot of guests to take care of. I can get it."

She excused herself and headed to the bar. A shiver crept across the back of her neck telling her his stare had followed her across the room.

She poured herself a glass of wine and studied the people at the party. They were all strangers to her, but Blake seemed to know everyone. Especially the women. She sipped her wine and watched him as he seemed to be pulled into one group then another. Everything about him radiated confidence and a magnetic sex appeal that had women flocking to him like ants to a picnic. He was unquestionably the most desirable man in the room. The most desirable man *she* had ever met.

She poured herself another drink. She didn't want to be a wet blanket or put a damper on his good time, so she stayed at the bar sipping her wine. Every now and then a couple would head upstairs, the most recent, a man with his hand firmly planted on the woman's ass and his erection blatantly obvious. She recalled Blake's mention of Tim's playroom. Is that where they were headed? How many couples were up there? Were they engaged in group sex? An orgy?

Was that the part of the house Tim had intended to show her on his *tour?*

Vicki wanted to get out of Tim's house and away from him as quickly as she could. She poured herself a third drink, fully aware of having too many drinks in too short a period of time. But the bar was the only place she felt safe. She didn't want to leave the openness of the area and have Tim corner her. A moment of panic slid over her, almost like a warning.

She looked for Blake and finally spotted him backed into a corner by the blonde from the volleyball game who was rubbing her big boobs against him. Genuine panic covered his face as he shot her a frantic look. Full blown jealousy grabbed her.

What the hell does that fucking bitch think she's doing with my man?

Total shock smacked her dead center. *My* man? Exactly what did that uncensored thought tell her?

"My pretty one." Tim sidled up to her and took her hand. "Allow me to give you that tour now."

"Uh, no, thank you." As soon as she opened her mouth and tried to talk, she knew she'd consumed her wine too quickly. "I need to find Blake. We, uh—"

"I believe he's busy at the moment." Tim glanced at Blake and the blonde. "It's rude of him to leave you alone like this. Allow me to keep you company."

He placed his hand at the small of her back and tried to steer her toward the stairs.

She pulled away, her manner more determined than polite this time. "No, thank you. I prefer to stay here."

"Oh, come on." Tim became more insistent. "There's no time like the present to take the grand tour."

"The lady said no." Blake clamped his hand on Tim's shoulder. His firm voice left no confusion about his intention.

A startled Tim took a step back.

"Sorry, Blake. You seemed busy." He glanced toward the blonde. "You deserted this delicious looking morsel so I thought I'd keep her company for you."

"That won't be necessary." Blake's stern expression said it all. He stood protectively in front of

Vicki as Tim made a hasty retreat. Turning toward her, Blake's voice and manner softened. He placed his hands on her shoulders. "Are you all right?"

"Yeah, I guess so. I mean, I might have had one too many glasses of wine. I ought to go home. You can, uh…" Vicki couldn't help herself as she turned to look at the blonde, then back at Blake. "You can stay with your friends if you want."

Even in her slightly impaired condition, she didn't want to exhibit any signs of jealousy. She had no right to dictate what he could and couldn't do regardless of her desires or her feelings for him. Jealousy was totally unacceptable. To admit jealousy was to admit her true feelings. It also used too much negative energy.

"Let's take a walk on the beach." He took her half-finished glass of wine from her hand and set it on the bar. "The fresh air will do you good."

"You don't need to take care of me. It's all right if you want to stay. I can make it home okay. After all, it's just next door."

"I don't want to stay here." Blake took her hand. "I've already had more than my fill of this party. I'd much rather take a walk with you, then go home."

"But won't Tim be unhappy if you leave so soon?"

"Tim can go fuck himself. I saw the way he was hitting on you, trying to get you upstairs to his playroom. As soon as I got Susie's silicone boobs pried off my chest, I came over here to pry Tim off of you."

"Oh, I thought she was your friend. I remember her being one of your volleyball partners. So, I just assumed…"

"Well…" He flashed her a comforting smile. "You assumed wrong. She's one of Tim's playmates, not mine."

"I feel so foolish." She took a calming breath.

"Don't." He squeezed her hand and brushed a tender kiss across her lips. "Come on, let's go."

Blake kept hold of her hand and headed directly to the door leading to the deck. He shot one last warning glance at Tim before stepping outside.

He put his arm around Vicki and steered her out onto the sand. They walked along the edge of the water, with Blake encouraging her to take deep breaths of the clean ocean air to help clear her head and stave off the effects of her last drink. They continued to walk for about half an hour before returning home. Once inside, he offered to make coffee.

"No, I'm fine now. That fresh air did the trick."

He kneeled next to where she sat on the sofa. "I owe you an apology."

"Why?" She seemed genuinely surprised. "An apology for what?"

"I never should have left your side. It started with a conversation with a man I've known for several years. I thought it would be a few minutes, and by that time Tim had pulled you onto the dance floor. I thought I'd be free by the time the song ended, but the night turned into a game of tug-of-war. Every time I tried to get away, someone else dragged me into conversation. Tim's a top notch attorney, but otherwise he's a real bastard. And Susie…I couldn't get her off me. She had those huge silicone melons shoved into my chest. I was about to tell her to fuck off."

"Maybe I'm the one who owes *you* an apology for being responsible for you leaving the party early, or at least earlier than you wanted."

"Don't even give that a thought. You have nothing to apologize for." He rose to his feet and held out his hand to assist her up from the sofa. "Come on, let's go to bed."

They climbed the stairs to the second floor. Blake wasn't sure what to do. He didn't want to take advantage of her if she'd had too much to drink. Not that he would really be taking advantage. After all, they hadn't been able to keep their hands off each other from day one. They had fucked in every room of the house at all times of the day and night. Whenever and wherever the desire hit them. Every time he saw her, he wanted her more than the last time, and her actions said she carried the same desires. But still, he didn't want her simply accommodating what she thought he wanted when she'd rather go to sleep.

He walked to her door. As much as he wanted to share his bed with her, he knew that if they did, then sleep would not be on the agenda. She looked tired. Beautiful, but tired. After helping her undress, he tucked her into her own bed and kissed her lovingly on the forehead. She had already fallen asleep.

"Good night, sweetheart," he whispered, not sure he should allow the words to escape into the open. "I'll see you in the morning. Have pleasant dreams."

Blake turned out the light, quietly left her room, and returned to his bedroom. He quickly undressed and climbed into bed. He wanted to rip Tim's head off when he saw the way the guy came on to Vicki and had attempted to herd her toward the stairs. Even though Blake knew he had no right to dictate who she should or shouldn't associate with, no way would he have allowed her to go upstairs with Tim.

His thoughts turned to the future. And the future he saw included Vicki. He found himself thinking about things that as recently as a week ago were totally out of the question. The word *love* frightened him. He had loved his son very much, and that loss nearly destroyed him. Taking a chance again truly frightened him. He couldn't bear the thought of giving his love and having something go wrong, of losing the person to whom he had given his heart. The thoughts and uncertainty swirled around inside his mind until he finally fell into an uneasy sleep.

Chapter Eight

As usual, Blake woke first thing in the morning. He made coffee, fed the cat, and cleaned the litter box. He wanted to give Vicki as much time to sleep as she wanted and needed. He brought in the Sunday newspaper and read it in the kitchen as he drank his coffee. The weather continued to be iffy, with sun one minute, clouds the next, and then periods of light rain. The forecast called for clearing that evening, followed by a warm, sunny week. He embraced the prospect of good beach weather and the chance to be outdoors.

After reading the newspaper, he refilled his coffee mug and carried it out onto the deck. He wanted to make his mind blank. To not concern himself with conflicting emotions. To not deal with what he'd come to recognize as a growing love for Vicki. Would his life ever become simple and uncomplicated? He couldn't continue the way he'd been for the last two years, simply existing on a day-to-day basis and refusing to think about tomorrow. The future had seemed so bleak, without meaning or purpose.

But now… Suddenly, the world seemed to have opened up for him. He had someone to care about, someone to cherish. And yes, someone to love. He couldn't deny it any longer. During the past week, against his most fervent intentions and in a shockingly short amount of time, he had ended up falling in love with Victoria Templeton—a woman with whom he seemingly had nothing in common other than hot and very satisfying sex.

Still, he couldn't shake the feeling of apprehension. What if something happened? What if it didn't work out? What if Vicki didn't love him the way he loved her? The possibility of taking a chance and having it backfire truly scared the hell out of him.

"I see you fed Ty-Ling."

He turned at the sound of her voice. She looked well rested. Her eyes sparkled, and her smile enchanted him. He couldn't stop the grin from turning up the corners of his mouth. "And the cat box, don't forget to mention I cleaned the furry little beast's bathroom. I want credit for all my good deeds."

"Duly noted."

She sat in one of the deck chairs, and he took the chair next to her. He studied her for a moment. "How are you feeling this morning?"

"Mostly, I'm feeling foolish." A hint of pink danced across her cheeks. "I think I owe you an apology. And, if I recall correctly, I wasn't very polite to Tim, either."

"You don't owe me an apology, and you most certainly don't owe Tim anything." A bit of a scowl crossed his face. "He behaved like the rutting pig he is, and you politely rebuffed him like the lady you are. You have no reason to be concerned about anything."

She turned to face him, uncertainty clouding her eyes. "Are you sure?"

"Positive. Just as I'm also sure I haven't said a proper good morning to you." He leaned his face close to hers and captured her mouth with a kiss more tender and caring than sensual. A kiss that grew in emotional depth with each passing second. The only physical contact between them continued to be just their lips. Neither reached out to hold the other, yet the very air sizzled with heated energy.

"Hope I'm not intruding." Tim's voice brought Vicki and Blake to attention.

Blake scrutinized his neighbor with a practiced eye. The obvious signs that Tim spent the night in his playroom couldn't be hidden, nor could his blood shot eyes and morning growth of beard. No question that he hadn't been to bed yet. Or more accurately, hadn't been to sleep yet.

"Isn't this a little early for you, Tim? What do you want?"

"Uh, well…I have the impression I might have upset you a little bit last night." His gaze shifted from Blake to Vicki. A touch of doubt darted through his eyes, accompanied by a bit of embarrassment. He returned his attention to Blake. "If I said or did anything you might have misinterpreted…well, I didn't mean to offend anyone. I was merely trying to be a gracious host."

"No harm done." Blake's flat tone said far more than his spoken words.

A blatantly ill-at-ease Tim awkwardly shifted his weight from one foot to the other. "I'd better get back home. I think there are still a couple of party goers sleeping it off upstairs. I have to get them out the door so I can catch a few hours sleep. I need to go into the office tomorrow. I'll see you later."

Vicki and Blake watched as Tim made his way next door. As soon as he entered his house, Blake turned toward her.

"Now, where were we?" He gently stroked her cheek with his fingertips. "Oh, yes. Now I remember."

"Hi, Blake."

He looked in the direction of the shout and saw Susie waving from Tim's deck. She was dressed only in the thong bottom of her swimsuit with her bare boobs bouncing in the morning sunlight. Her blonde hair was in wild disarray, attesting to a night of wanton sex. Before he could say anything, she jiggled her way across the sand to his deck. When she drew close, he could see red bite marks around her nipples and several hickeys not quite covered by the front of her thong.

"You look like you had a busy night." He arched a brow. "Don't you think you should find the top to your swimsuit before you go prancing down the beach? You don't want to get arrested for indecent exposure again, do you?"

"I don't know where it is. I think someone must have stolen it."

"Tim will help you find it. If not, get one of his T-shirts to put on."

"I thought maybe you'd have something I could wear." Susie eyed him coyly, ran the tip of her tongue across her upper lip, and thrust out her silicon chest.

"Sorry. You'd better hurry next door before Tim falls asleep."

No mistaking the disappointment on her face and the practiced pout as she stuck out her lower lip. When she turned to walk back to Tim's house, the sight that greeted Vicki and Blake nearly had them falling off their chairs as they tried to hold back their laughter. Someone had taken an ink marker to Susie's ass cheeks and had written *I love to fuck* in large red letters.

Blake brushed a tender kiss across Vicki's lips. "One thing's for sure, they can't get her for false advertising."

"Maybe we should go inside before more of Tim's party stragglers find their way over here. Besides, I need to refill my coffee cup."

"Excellent suggestion."

Blake followed Vicki into the kitchen. He refilled her cup, then gestured toward the newspaper.

"I've already read the morning paper, but I left it for you. I checked the movie listings to see what's playing at the village theater. Would you like to take in a matinee this afternoon? There's a mystery showing that's gotten good reviews."

"That sounds like fun. A late afternoon showing, then some dinner?"

"And in the meantime…" He stood behind her, wrapped his arms around her waist, and kissed the side of her neck. "I didn't have an opportunity to give you a proper good night before you fell asleep. So, maybe before the movie…"

"I knew there was something missing when I woke up this morning. My first clue—being in *my* bed. And my second clue—being there alone."

Vicki leaned against his chest. Even though they'd made love yesterday afternoon, they had not made love last night or that morning, either. It had been all her fault, and she fully intended to make it up to him.

A sensual warmth spread across her skin when his hands slipped under her T-shirt to cup her breasts. They certainly weren't as big as those jugs of Susie's, but from all indications, Blake liked what she had to offer.

And she liked it when he touched her. She liked everything about him. This kite flying beach bum with the sexy sun bleached streaks in his dark blond hair and no job was the same man who made her heart sing. The man with whom she might be falling in love.

The man with whom she had perhaps *already* fallen in love.

"I have a little surprise I think you'll find entertaining." His seductive whisper sent a shiver of delight rippling across her skin.

"I have a little surprise for you, too. One I think you'll find fascinating, and I hope very exciting." The idea had occurred to her in the shower that morning, an idea that had come to fruition when the tantalizing fragrance of his shower gel stimulated her senses.

He turned her in his arms, placed a quick kiss on her lips, then grasped her hand. "Shall we go upstairs and share our surprises?"

Blake led her into his bedroom, quickly peeled off his clothes, and sat on the edge of the bed, but Vicki didn't hurry to get undressed. He tugged on her hand until she stood next to him. "I can't think of a better way to spend a lazy morning than exploding in a frenzy of passion. I'll share my surprise with you if you're a good girl."

Blake pulled her T-shirt over her head and dropped it on the floor next to his clothes. As he tongued her nipple, he thought about the brand new, unopened jar of chocolate body paint he'd brought home from Tim's party.

"Mmm, I always try to be a good girl." She closed her eyes as the smile curled the corners of her mouth.

His breath caught in his lungs. "I'll definitely give

you a gold star for being good. In fact, I'll give you four gold stars out of four for being even better than incredibly good." His voice turned raspy with his ragged breathing. "And just as soon as you get out of the rest of these clothes, I'll let you show me just how good you are."

"Now we come to my surprise." She unsnapped her jeans and lowered the zipper, then stopped. Her sexy grin said she wanted him to finish undressing her, a task he would perform with pleasure. He tugged her jeans down her legs, she stepped out of them, and he dropped them on top of the other discarded clothes. She stood naked except for her black lace bikini panties. He paused to drink in her beauty. Her glossy chestnut hair hung almost to her shoulders, framing her delicately sculpted features. Her hazel eyes sparkled with passion. His cock already stood at full attention. His hand trembled slightly as he inched the panties down her hips.

Blake's blue eyes widened in shock, then glowed with excitement as he sucked in a hard breath. "That's fucking incredible! And so very sexy." A hint of huskiness crept into his voice. "If I wasn't already undressed and fully charged, that's a sight that would have me rock-hard in an instant and my cock fighting to get free of my clothes. I don't know what prompted you to do this, but I hope you keep doing it."

Vicki had shaved her mound, leaving only the curls that formed a heart shape. The feel of the razor gliding sensually through the lather had sent tremors of excitement coursing through her body and left her pussy tingling with a newfound sensation. After rinsing away the lather and hair, she admired her handiwork in the mirror. She made a few minor touch ups, very pleased with the final results. Her inner muscles had clenched in anticipation as she imagined Blake's reaction when he saw it.

She'd started to touch her excited clit, but stopped herself in time. No, she wouldn't take a chance on triggering an orgasm as a result of her own touch. She wanted her first orgasm with her heart-shaped muff to be Blake's doing. It had been all she could do to sit still and drink her coffee while waiting for the opportunity to let him uncover her little secret. And the fire of passion burning in his eyes told her how much he liked what he saw.

"I'm glad you approve." She shivered slightly when he traced the outline of the heart with his fingertip.

He wrapped his arms around her hips and pulled her to him. His warm breath ruffled through the curls on her newly decorated mound. "You are so exquisite." His words came out barely above a whisper. "If I live to be a hundred years old, and you grant me the privilege of providing you pleasure each and every day, I still won't have my fill of you."

A deeply felt, yet confusing emotional jolt raced through her body. His professed need was the last thing she expected to hear. And maybe the last thing she *wanted* to hear. He had already turned her carefully planned future into shambles. She hadn't thought there was any room in her life for this kite flying beach bum with no plan for the future. But just as she needed water and air to exist, she also needed Blake Callahan to feel truly alive. Not wanting it to be so did not change that reality.

Tremors of delight washed over her when he flicked the tip of his tongue back and forth across her clit. She emitted an excited moan as the sensations took control of her body. He seemed to instinctively know just how and where to touch her, when to lick, and when to suck.

Levels of intensity built on top of one another as she spiraled into her orgasm...her first orgasm with her new look. Other ideas popped into her mind—like maybe getting a seductive little tattoo on her inner thigh, nipple rings, or even a gold ring through her pussy lip. She dismissed the errant thoughts as totally impractical, except maybe clip on nipple rings, but decided to forget the piercings other than her already pierced ears. Hmm, maybe she could get one little tattoo, though.

Her knees grew weak. She wouldn't be able to support her own weight much longer. But she didn't want to break off the marvelous things his mouth was doing to her pussy even long enough to climb into bed.

Blake's chest heaved with his labored breathing. No question about it. He had become totally addicted to her, to the texture of her pussy lips, to her taste, to the way her engorged clit quivered and throbbed in response to his tongue and lips, to her pussy walls wrapping his cock in a tight sheath that felt like hot, wet velvet, to her muscles tugging and squeezing his shaft...and now the heart shape shaved on her mound. Definitely the sexiest thing he'd ever seen on a woman. Sexy and classy. Not outlandish and garish like some women were with their sexual adornments.

And that was just the physical.

The way she touched his carefully guarded

vulnerability stirred his closed off emotions until they rose to the surface. Forcing him to think beyond today and allowing him to get a glimpse of what tomorrow could be with the right woman.

Her body quivered as orgasmic tremors raced through her. His mouth filled with the taste he craved. The taste hers alone. He fell backward with his legs dangling over the edge of the bed and brought her with him, positioning her so she straddled his shoulders. She had shared her surprise with him, and now it was his turn. He sucked on her clit for a couple of seconds, immediately enveloped in the throes of her orgasm. She was the most exquisite woman he had ever known.

He eased his mouth away from her hot pussy. A look of disappointment flashed through her eyes.

"You've treated me to your surprise." His words came out in a raspy whisper. "And it was incredible...beautiful and tantalizing. Now, it's my turn."

He moved her off his chest, leaned over to the nightstand, and took a jar from the drawer.

"This is the one good thing that came from Tim's party last night." He held the jar up for her to see and extended a wicked little grin. "Chocolate body paint."

"Really?" Desire glowed in the depths of her eyes. She took the jar from him and read the label. "Mmm, it says it's edible. What a delicious thought. And I know just how to serve it."

She broke the seal on the jar, removed the lid, and sniffed the contents. "Smells good." She took some on her finger and put it in her mouth. "Tastes good, too."

"So, it passes your inspection? I wasn't sure which flavor to take. Tim also had cinnamon, cherry, and mint. But I decided everyone loves chocolate."

"Chocolate is definitely my preference." A sexy smile lit her face. "Just relax. This won't hurt a bit."

Vicki slowly and sensually covered his erection with the body paint until not a speck of skin showed. Then she covered his balls. She licked her lips. His cock unadorned had been a thing of beauty from the moment she'd first seen it standing hard, thick, and tall. And now, covered in one of her favorite treats? Absolutely irresistible.

"My, my, my, that definitely looks like the kind of chocolate covered lollipop that deserves to be licked clean."

A long slow swipe of her tongue started at the base and moved up the underside of his shaft to the tip, setting the pace for what would come next. Each lap of her tongue along his length removed a little more of the chocolate. And each foray elicited a low moan of delight from him that tantalized her senses. Blake Callahan's chocolate covered cock...what a terrific combination of treats. A delicious late morning snack to be savored and not rushed.

Her pussy tingled with excitement as each flick of chocolate disappeared into her mouth. She ran her hands across his chest, her fingers touching the hard planes of his sculpted body. Everything about him excited her more than she thought possible, more than she believed could ever be.

Slowly, sensually, the chocolate disappeared, first from his cock, and then from his balls. His tense muscles and deep growls told her how much he enjoyed her attentions. And she loved providing him with the pleasure just as she reveled in the ecstasy he gave her.

"Hand me that jar." Blake's husky voice carried all the desire flowing through his body. "I see something that would taste great covered in chocolate."

He situated her on her back in the middle of the bed, her legs spread in an inviting manner. He painted the outline of her heart shaped curls, her clit, and pussy lips, then fully covered her breasts and added an extra dollop of chocolate on each nipple. He studied his handiwork for a moment, then gave another blob of chocolate to her clit. His sexy grin appeared, a grin she adored because it said pure lust and hedonism coursed through his veins and filled his thoughts. Something that always resulted in intense multiple orgasms for her.

"That definitely looks good enough to eat." He drew in a deep breath, held it a moment, and then slowly exhaled. "And just visualizing that heart shape in my mind is enough to make my dick stand up and beg for attention."

He flicked his tongue along the outline, licking the chocolate away from the design. His raspy words barely made it into the open. "You are so fucking incredible...so beautiful...so exciting..." He sucked some of the chocolate from her engorged clit, then flashed her a lewd grin. "And so tasty, too."

His words stopped when he buried his face between her legs, licking her pussy lips and sucking her clit until all the chocolate had disappeared. And each stroke of his tongue, each movement of his lips, sent orgasmic tremors through her body. Convulsive waves of total ecstasy assaulted her senses, one after another, until she didn't know how much more her body could absorb. She became light-headed, fearing she might actually faint from the pure unbridled rapture.

Blake grabbed one of the condoms from the top of the nightstand and quickly rolled it on. He wanted to bury his cock in her inviting pussy. He *needed* it inside that hot, wet cocoon. He managed to maintain his control as he penetrated her one slow inch at a time, until his dick had become fully embedded in her tunnel. A low rumble of intense pleasure clawed its way out of his throat. No one had ever given him greater physical pleasure than she did when he made love to her. Each time became more thrilling than the last, more intense physically, more enthralling—and emotionally overwhelming.

He licked the chocolate from her breasts and sucked it from her nipples. All the while, he kept up a smooth rhythm of delving into her and pulling back, then shoving in again. She met each of his down strokes with an upward thrust of her hips. They moved in harmony, completely attuned to each other's needs and desires. Stroke after stroke, the excitement built. He pumped harder and faster. She urged him on with her response, matching his increased level of fervor with zeal. He captured her mouth in a demanding kiss, his tongue darting in and exploring and her tongue meshing with his in an ancient mating ritual. Each flooding the other's mouth with the tantalizing taste of chocolate.

Multiple orgasms rippled through her pussy. She tightened her hold on him, moving her legs from his hips upward to encircle his waist. Her hands played across his tautly muscled back, moving erratically each time he plunged his marvelous cock into her depths. He gave one final deep thrust, then his body shuddered with hard spasms.

They continued to make love. Sometimes in a

heated frenzy of passion. Sometimes slow and loving. Sex would give way to periods of quiet togetherness, words being unnecessary. Then the embers would burst into incendiary sparks, igniting their passions again until exhaustion finally claimed them. They held each other, reveling in the blissful contentment of total and complete satisfaction.

Blake's addiction to her had gotten another fix, but it only made him want more. Breakfast, lunch, and dinner. Morning, noon, and night. Anywhere and everywhere. Any way and every way. His thoughts tried to turn to what would happen when it came time for her to move on, to pursue the rest of her declared agenda of living on campus and getting her master's degree. He shook away the thoughts. To deal with them would mean he needed to face his own future, to make a decision about returning to his faculty position as a department head at the same university.

It meant he would need to acknowledge the future and make decisions about his place in the scheme of things. He forced the confusion aside. He wasn't ready to deal with it, at least not yet.

He pulled his still half-hard dick from her pussy and folded her in his embrace. Her eyes sparkled with a combination of contentment and desire. She exuded a passion that reached out to him. The pink flush of orgasm covered her damp face in a beauty that touched his senses on all levels. Perhaps he wasn't ready to deal with the future yet, but he could no longer stop it from seeping into his thoughts. And the future seemed to be synonymous with Victoria Templeton.

She snuggled into his arms as naturally as if she had been doing it for years rather than barely over a week. She gently fondled his balls. He placed a tender kiss on her lips to let her know how much he enjoyed her touch. And he continued to hold her, to bask in a contentment he hadn't known since the day his son died. It all felt so right.

Morning had become afternoon. The movie they wanted to see started in an hour. He brushed a soft kiss across her mouth. "I'll race you to the shower to see who gets to use it first." His sexy grin spread across his face. "Unless you want to save time by showering together."

"You know as well as I do that showering together may save water, but it definitely won't save any time." She flicked the tip of her tongue against his lower lip. "In fact, there's only one place *that* can lead, and it's not into the village to see a movie."

"You're right." But instead of getting out of bed, he slipped a finger between her pussy lips and wiggled it inside her.

She let out a soft moan, closed her eyes, and allowed the sensation to wash over her for a moment. Then she batted at his hand. "That's not going to get us to the movies, either."

"Once again, you're right. I'll let you shower first." He sat up and glanced out the window. "Looks like the storm clouds have cleared off. We can walk into the village."

"I won't be long." She scooted out of bed and headed toward the bathroom.

****

Vicki and Blake casually strolled hand-in-hand the two blocks back to the house after enjoying an early dinner at a quaint little Italian restaurant following the movie. They talked quietly as they walked along the street. When they arrived home, he poured two glasses of wine and carried them out onto the deck where they watched the sky turn from sunset to night. Down the beach, the lights from the businesses along the pier shone brightly. Faint music floated on the air from somewhere up the beach.

She finally broke the silence, not because it was uncomfortable but because there had been something on her mind for the last hour.

"Tomorrow is Monday. I'm going to file a police report about Mr. Edwards then I'll be in my office working. Do you have any plans for the day?"

"I really haven't given it any thought. I guess I'll work with my stunt kites and see if I can come up with a routine so I can enter the contest." He glanced over at her. "Why do you ask?"

"No particular reason. It's just that I've never spent time around someone who didn't have a job or any type of standard routine during the work week. I wasn't sure what you normally did with your time."

Her words sent warning signals to Blake, setting his senses on alert. What kind of hidden meaning lurked behind her question? On one hand, he had to admit his life had become a daily routine in which he didn't accomplish anything, as if he had no purpose anymore. But for two years he had been content to settle for that. Just get through today without thinking about tomorrow. Now, however, her question caused a ripple of something he couldn't quite identify—part resentment, part guilt. It had been a valid question, but that didn't mean he wanted to face it.

She had become more important to him than he'd

ever believed anyone could, and at a lightning speed that literally boggled the mind and took his breath away nearly as much as she did. He had already lost someone who meant more to him than life itself. He couldn't handle it happening again. Two starkly different realities poised on the brink of battle.

He stared out at the ocean, making it obvious to Vicki that she wouldn't be getting any more of a response to her question than he'd already given, almost as if he were afraid to answer it. Something very personal remained hidden deep inside him, something he didn't want to share. Intellectually, she understood and accepted that, but emotionally she felt shut out, as if he had closed a door on her and refused to share what he kept locked behind it.

A cool breeze wafted across the deck, sending a shiver rippling over her skin.

"It's a little chilly out here." She set her wine glass on the small table and stood. "I'm going to put on a sweater. I'll be right back."

Somewhere in the back of her mind she knew the shiver was due to more than just the temperature. Blake seemed to be suddenly pulling away from her, and she didn't know why. Had their relationship been nothing more than hot, heavy sex, which he felt had run its course? Had he decided it had been a mistake to ask her to stay in his house for the summer?

She climbed the stairs to the second floor. An uncomfortable sensation of foreboding closed in around her. A sound from Blake's bedroom interrupted her mounting panic. She stopped at his door and flipped on the light switch. "Ty-Ling! What have you done?"

The cat scampered from the top of Blake's dresser

and darted out the door, leaving the contents of an overturned box scattered on the floor.

Vicki rushed inside to clean up the cat's mess. She grabbed the various papers, a video disc, several photographs, and placed them back in the box. All except one. The photograph showed Blake and a little boy who looked to be about six years-old. After placing the box on top of the dresser, she sat on the edge of his bed and stared at the picture. She turned it over to see if anything was written on the back. All she saw was a date indicating the photo had been taken two and a half years ago. Who was the little boy? A relative? A friend's child?

"What the hell are you doing?" Blake's angry voice sliced through the air, cutting off her thoughts. She jerked to attention and found an equally furious looking Blake standing in the doorway scowling at her. He crossed the room in several quick, long strides and grabbed the photograph from her hands. He placed it in the box with everything else, then put the container on the top shelf of his closet.

He whirled and faced her. "Why were you going through my personal belongings?"

"I—I wasn't. It was on the floor—"

"Stay out of my things." He snapped out the words as if not even aware she'd been talking, then turned and ran down the stairs. She heard the outside door open and slam shut…then silence.

Her insides collapsed into a jumbled mess, as if he'd slammed the door shut on whatever future they might have had together. Tears welled in her eyes and trickled down her cheeks. She wiped them away with the back of her hand. The last thing she wanted to do was cry. But she didn't seem to be able to stop or control the tremors. A sick churning knotted in the pit of her stomach. She couldn't have been more stunned if he had actually struck her. Nor could she have been suffering more anguish or been in any greater emotional pain.

She glanced at the box on the closet shelf. What did it contain that had caused such an irrational, angry outburst? More tears ran down her cheeks, only this time she didn't make any effort to wipe them away. Wave after wave of raw pain crashed through her body, draining her of all energy. Whatever that box contained, it was obviously an issue for him. As much as she wanted to know what was in it, she resisted the urge to take it from the shelf.

She tried to assemble her thoughts into a pragmatic mode, to brush aside her pain and focus on the problem at hand. Somehow she had to force Blake to listen to her explanation, to make him understand she hadn't been prying into his life or snooping in his personal belongings. But how?

She tried to stand up, but her legs had turned to lead. After finally struggling to her feet, she retreated to her bedroom. What to think? What to do? How to make him listen? She had too many questions and no answers. She tried to inject some calm into the sudden chaos that had erupted around her, but without much success. In the past, she'd been able to maintain her strong determination without any difficulty once she set her mind on a course of action.

She'd always known exactly what she wanted out of life and how to get there. Hard work and dedication to her chosen course of action had been her credo. Then suddenly this man had turned her carefully planned life upside down. Even thinking straight had become a formidable task. Whatever he had chosen to lock away inside him had to somehow be tied to the contents of the box.

After gulping in several steadying breaths, she squared her shoulders and set her resolve. One way or another, she'd make him listen to her explanation about why she was in his bedroom holding the photograph, even if she had to tie him to a chair. According to the standards she'd set for her life and had always believed were important, Blake Callahan was wrong for her in every way. So why did everything about him feel so right?

She had no intention of allowing him to slip through her fingers due to nothing more than some stupid misunderstanding. She hurried downstairs, adamant about forcing him to hear what she had to say. But, to her dismay, he was nowhere to be found, not in the house or on the deck. His car was in the garage, so wherever he'd gone couldn't be all that far away since he was on foot.

Vicki returned to the deck, plopped into her chair, and picked up the glass of wine she'd left there before going upstairs. He wasn't going to escape her that easily. He had to come home eventually, and she would be waiting for him.

Regardless of what kind of an attitude he chose to display, no matter how angry he seemed to be, she would make him listen.

Chapter Nine

Blake slowed his pace, then finally came to a halt. He bent forward with his hands on his thighs and gulped in deep breaths. He'd jogged down the beach on the bike path for over a mile, going well beyond the pier. Total confusion continued to swirl through his mind along with anger, hurt, guilt, shame, embarrassment, and some other emotions he couldn't even identify. Lashing out at Vicki, losing his temper when he'd seen her holding the photograph of his son, had been a stupid knee-jerk reaction.

She had no way of knowing what the contents of the box meant to him. She had tried to tell him something, but he'd only compounded his fuck-up by storming out of the room without listening to her. He never should have done that, either. It was totally unacceptable behavior, especially toward someone he cared about as much as he cared for Vicki.

Cared about. The words were wholly inadequate to accurately describe his feelings for her. But the word *love* still scared him. A little over a week ago, he hadn't even known Vicki existed. No one falls in love in a week. They develop an infatuation, yes. Lust, most definitely. But love? Yet, he felt as if he had known her for a lifetime.

He straightened and stared out at the ocean. The full moon shimmered across the water, casting a silvery glow over everything. Thoughts of Vicki flooded his mind. Memories assaulted every fiber of his existence. Her touch, her taste, her scent, the sound of her voice, waking in the morning with her sleeping in his arms, just knowing she was near. Somehow he had to make things right. But could he do that without committing to a relationship? Just the thought of commitment sent a cold shiver rippling across his skin.

This compulsively organized woman with every minute of her life planned out and noted in her schedule book, this woman who thought only of tomorrow while sacrificing today, had done what no one else had been able to do. She'd forced him to think about the future. A future that included her as part of his life. But how far was he willing to go to make it happen? How much of a change was he willing—or able—to accept?

Or maybe the real question was whether he was even capable of changing. Had his future become firmly set in concrete? A lonely future without that special someone to share all the love he had locked away? A future without Vicki?

He headed back to the house, this time at a slow walk. He desperately needed to clear his head, to put things in proper perspective. His emotions left him torn between two extremes—his fear of the future on one hand, and his all-consuming need to have Vicki as a permanent part of his life on the other side of the equation. A permanent part of his life meant beyond the confines of only today without consideration for tomorrow. And it also meant telling her about his son, about what had happened. Revealing his most hidden secret, deepest pain, and greatest vulnerability.

And that required trusting her with his wounded

heart.

He put one foot in front of the other, each step bringing him closer to the moment of truth, closer to facing his own demons. He forced everything from his mind, everything except the sound of the waves breaking along the shore. One step at a time until he saw the house. He came to an abrupt halt.

The only visible light shone from Vicki's bedroom window on the second floor. The other windows and the deck were dark. A nervous jitter twisted in the pit of his stomach. Talking to her could not be put off any longer. He needed to tell her tonight even if he had to wake her up to do it.

The sudden realization slammed into his consciousness. The possibility of losing Vicki frightened him even more than exposing his pain.

Blake picked up his pace as he crossed the sand toward the stairs leading to the deck. But it wasn't until he reached the top step that he realized she was sitting there in the dark. He hesitated, not sure what to say. The possibility of her being there had not occurred to him. He thought he had a few more minutes before he needed to face the truth. A few more minutes to choose just the right words to say.

Vicki took the initiative and spoke before he had a chance to say anything. "I've been waiting for you to get back. I want to explain—"

"There's no—"

"Don't interrupt me." She snapped out the order making no effort to hide her displeasure. "You're going to listen to what I have to say." Nervousness clung to her words. She took a deep breath, held it, then slowly exhaled. "I was *not* snooping in your things. On my way to my room, I heard a noise in your room. I turned on the light and saw that Ty-Ling had knocked a box off your dresser, and the contents had spilled onto the floor. I shooed her away and put everything back into the box, all except that one photograph. It caught my attention, and I was wondering who the little boy was when you came in. That's exactly what happened, nothing more. I would never snoop in your belongings."

"I'm sorry." He remained on the top step with his foot poised on the deck. Waves of guilt crashed through him. "I apologize for yelling at you. I had no right to jump to conclusions. And when you tried to say something…well, I was totally out of line."

"You certainly were." A hard edge rode her voice.

He had hurt her with his words and actions, something he deeply regretted. Forcing himself to move, he found the empty chair next to her. Offering her an embarrassed and somewhat stilted smile, he tried to sound casual. "Do you mind if I sit down?"

"It's your house. Sit wherever you want."

He flinched at the sting of her words, especially her reference to it being *his* house. They sat in silence for what seemed like eternity before he finally broke the uncomfortable silence. "I believe I owe you an explanation, rather than the other way around."

"You don't *owe* me anything." She rose from the chair. "Now, if you'll excuse me, I'm going to bed." She turned and started for the door.

He grabbed her hand, bringing her to a halt. "No…I've given this a lot of thought." He forced her back into her chair but didn't let go of her hand. He needed the comfort of her touch before he could continue, something to bolster his courage before digging into the deep well of his despair. "I don't know where we're headed, what type of relationship we have, or what you want or expect, but nothing can go forward unless you know the truth. I can't hold it inside any longer."

Never in his life had he been as unsure about what to say or do as at that moment. He swallowed the lump in his throat and forced out the words before they died in his mouth. "It started nearly nine years ago. A woman I had been casually dating informed me she was pregnant. I did the honorable thing and married her even though I didn't love her." He sucked in a steadying breath in an attempt to settle his nerves. "Shortly after our son was born, she announced she didn't want to be tied down to a baby or stuck in a lousy marriage. She abandoned both of us. I got a divorce and raised my son on my own. He was the joy of my life. Each day was an exciting new adventure. I received so much pleasure from seeing the world anew through his eyes. Having him helped erase the bitterness of my marriage.

"He loved the beach. We'd come here in summer and winter. When he was three years-old, I taught him how to fly a kite. He took to it like a duck to water. For the next three years, it was the activity we most enjoyed together. Then one day, one terrible day…" Pain ripped through his chest and choked off his words for a couple of seconds. "That horrible day a reckless driver ran him down right in front of me. Killed him instantly. That image burned into my mind and has never gone away. Something inside me died along with my son. That's when it hit me that there was no tomorrow, only today. Live each day for what it has to offer because no one is guaranteed a tomorrow. And for two years, that's what I've been doing."

Tears welled in Vicki's eyes as she listened to Blake talk of his son. She brought his hand to her lips and kissed it, then held it tightly against her chest. She literally felt his pain as if it were her own.

Everything made sense now. His actions, his lifestyle, the kites. If only she had known. She had never felt closer to anyone than she did to Blake right now. The intensity of the sex, the emotional strings, all of it had led her down a path she'd never trod before with any man. But it almost paled in comparison to the bond that had just been forged between them. She had just given herself permission to do what she'd already done, fall totally and completely in love with Blake Callahan.

"Is there anything I can do to help? Do you want to talk about it, or would you rather keep your memories to yourself? I'm here for whatever you want."

"You've already done more than I thought possible." He kept hold of her hand and brought it to his lips. "You've forced me to think about the future, about what it holds. About where my life is going and where it needs to go. About what my future can be. For two years, I've only been going through the motions on the outside while dying on the inside. Now, for the first time since the darkness of that nightmare descended over me, I can see daylight. I feel a spark of life inside me, and it's taking hold, becoming a flame."

For the first time since sitting in the chair, he turned to face her. "Thank you for giving me a glimpse of the future, for showing me what can be. It's been a long time since I looked at all the items in my keepsake box. I'd like to share them with you…if you'd like to see them."

"Yes, I'd like that very much. I'd be honored to have you share them with me."

Vicki and Blake went upstairs to his bedroom where he retrieved the box from the closet shelf. They sat on the edge of the bed, and he showed her each of the precious memories he'd stored for safe keeping. Minutes turned into an hour, which became two hours.

Blake finally returned each of the items to the box and set it on the dresser. The experience had been a freeing catharsis for him, a horrendous weight lifted from his shoulders. A time of closure for the emotional trauma that had been eating him alive for two long years. The confusion that had run rampant through his mind from the day Vicki first opened his front door had finally been cleared away. He'd found that perfect someone to share both his joys and sorrows. Someone he could love with all his heart.

The very air around them seemed to glow with unspoken love. He folded Vicki in his embrace, holding her tightly against him. She responded by slipping her arms around his waist and nestling her head against his shoulder. They swayed together, as if moving to some unheard music. He caressed her shoulders, then ran his hand down to her hip.

Everything flowed in natural progression. Pieces of clothing fell to the floor. He snuggled her into his king size bed and captured her mouth with a tender kiss that conveyed the love coursing through his veins. They shared the truth of a deep and abiding love rather than heated frenzy.

Vicki wrapped her leg around his as she skimmed

her fingers across his back and down to his firm ass. She welcomed the sensation of his tongue brushing hers, their textures meshing in a seductive ritual. Everything about Blake Callahan excited her physically, and now they shared an emotional bond— the trust he'd placed in her by telling her about his son.

Her core clenched when he inserted his finger, eliciting a soft moan of pleasure from her. A tingle of excitement rippled through her body. More than sex filled the air, more than the physical rush of primal need. She melted into his touch as he slipped his finger in and out while stimulating her clit. His dick stood tall and ready. She wrapped her hand around his girth and stroked his length. Gently. Tenderly. Lovingly.

Every nuance of their coupling spoke of the love neither had yet verbalized, a love each had been too afraid to acknowledge. A joyous love that had started with an incendiary spark of heated physical desire and became a full blown blaze of all-consuming need.

Blake rolled on a condom and situated himself between her legs. Once again the love he felt for her flowed through his kiss. He entered her, slowly delving into the depths of her pussy until his cock was fully embedded. Time ceased to have any meaning as they shared an intimacy every bit as emotional as physical.

He increased his pace, and Vicki met each of his down strokes with an upward thrust of her hips. Waves of euphoria spiraled out of control as she tightened her legs around his waist. Convulsions claimed her. A moment later, his release shuddered through his body. The orgasmic climax far exceeded their previous sexual encounters. This one was personal, so very personal. It carried a strong emotional connection that exceeded the physical.

They made love again, two bodies in complete harmony. Two souls twined into one loving entity.

****

Blake opened his eyes to the golden hues of a beautiful sunrise with the most beautiful woman he had ever known nestled in his arms. A woman he wanted to spend the rest of his life making happy. He placed a gentle kiss on her forehead.

The future suddenly held all sorts of promise. Maybe even the possibility of a second chance at a family. How did Vicki feel about children? She'd never mentioned anything about wanting a family. Everything with her had been totally career oriented. Even though they were living together, their arrangement had been clearly established as a temporary situation for the summer only. At the end of the season she planned to move on, to return to school for her master's degree. She had made it clear up front that she was all business.

Of course, a lot of things had happened since that first day. Would she be interested in permanently settling into domestic co-habitation? Were his thoughts and considerations beyond the scope of reality?

Vicki stirred and slowly opened her eyes. A totally captivating smile lit her face when her gaze landed on him. "Good morning."

"Good morning to you, too." He brushed a gentle kiss across her lips. "Did you sleep well?"

"Perfectly." She snuggled closer to him and closed her eyes. A contented smile turned up the corners of her mouth as she ran her hand along his thigh.

A soft moan escaped his throat. "You keep that up, and we won't be getting out of bed until lunchtime."

"I can think of far worse ways to spend a morning, but…" She opened her eyes and sat up. "I played hooky all weekend, and now I have to pay the price. I have lots to do today."

Disappointment nipped at Blake. Monday morning, and time to go to work. She had taught him that tomorrow existed. Would he be able to convince her that today was just as important? He climbed out of bed and allowed her first use of the bathroom. Even though there was a full bath downstairs, he chose to wait until she finished.

After showering and dressing, Vicki fixed breakfast. Blake cleaned up and loaded the dishwater when they finished eating as she settled into her office in the dining room. She still needed to go to the police station and file a complaint. It had been a delightful weekend of carefree fun and incredible sex. And it had ended with the type of emotional bonding she had never believed could be possible with a man who meant everything to her. But now it was back to reality and the need to earn a living.

What a strange turn of events. Rather than being anxious to get to work, she wished it were still Sunday morning. With a little sigh of resignation, she turned her attention to the matter at hand. After turning on her computer, she sorted through what needed to be done. But no matter how hard she tried, she couldn't keep her mind on work. Her thoughts continually strayed to Blake and what he had said before he told her about his son. His words about not knowing what kind of relationship they had or what she wanted continued to play through her mind. She wasn't sure what she wanted, either. She knew she wanted Blake, but beyond that she couldn't lock on to any solid thoughts.

All of her energy had been spent working toward a secure future. Yet, suddenly, it didn't seem as important to her anymore.

She forced her attention to her work and soon became engrossed in the functions of the day. The sound of the doorbell grabbed her attention. She glanced at the clock, surprised that two hours had passed. Blake had gone outside, so she went to answer the door.

The postman handed her a large manila envelope. "Delivery here for Callahan. Needs to be signed for."

After signing the receipt and closing the door, Vicki looked at the mailing label. The name on the envelope jumped out at her. *Dr. Edward B. Callahan, Jr.* The return address was the university. She scrunched up her nose as confusion swirled through her mind. Who was the envelope intended for? A relative of Blake's? Someone he was expecting to see? Someone who would be stopping by to pick up his mail? Was the doctor a medical designation or, since it came from the university, an educational degree? Could the person it was intended for be on staff at the university?

Taking the envelope with her, she went to her office and pulled out her university catalogue. She turned to the section with photographs of the faculty.

Her gaze locked on the photograph above the name of Dr. Edward B. Callahan, Jr. Blake. Her heart skipped a beat, and the breath froze in her lungs. The catalogue further identified Dr. Callahan as head of the Sociology Department.

Her legs trembled with shock and refused to support her. She fell back into her chair. How could this be? The beach bum who had turned her life upside down had a PhD and held the prestigious position of department head at the university? He had cast all of that aside in favor of…of what? To fly kites on the beach?

Vicki didn't know what to think or what to do. She'd been confused before, but that was nothing compared to the total bewilderment that now assaulted her senses. The shock slowly ebbed, leaving an odd numbness in its wake. She continued to stare at the photograph, unable to move or think.

"Vicki?"

The sound of her name brought her out of her stupor. She looked up and saw Blake standing in the doorway.

He slowly walked around the table toward her. "Is something wrong?"

"The postman just delivered this." With a trembling hand, she held out the envelope. "I signed for it. It's addressed to—to Dr. Edward B. Callahan, Jr., and it's from the university. I looked in my university catalogue and…" She held it up for him to see the faculty picture. She didn't know what to say.

He took the envelope from her. "I've always used my middle name to separate my identity from my father's." The words came out softly, almost in a whisper, as if he didn't want to acknowledge her discovery.

Blake opened the envelope and pulled out the papers. After quickly skimming the cover letter, he returned everything to the envelope.

"Can you imagine my shock when the picture in my university catalogue of Dr. Callahan turned out to be *you?*" Hurt welled inside her. "Why didn't you tell me?" A sob caught in her throat. "Why did you keep your background such a secret? You've accomplished something to be very proud of. Not only a doctoral degree, but head of a department. After all that hard work, you just threw it away—"

His shocked expression stopped her in mid-sentence. A mixed sensation churned in the pit of her stomach—hurt that he would have kept that knowledge from her, disappointment that he would throw away such a promising career, and finally panic at the realization that she sounded callous about his grief over the death of his son. She tried to force out some words, an apology or an explanation…something. But nothing came out of her mouth.

"I tried to cope with my son's death, but each day became more and more difficult to deal with." His voice carried no emotion, not a hint of what was going on inside him. "I had to get away. About six months ago, I put in for a sabbatical. I sold my house close to the university and ended up here. Now they want me to cut my sabbatical short and return right away."

He didn't say anything else. He simply took the envelope, walked out of the room, and went upstairs, leaving her in stunned silence. She wanted to go after him, to say she was sorry for how unfeeling her comments must have sounded. But on the other hand, perhaps it would be better if she waited a while, gave him some time to himself. The letter from the university obviously presented him with a new situation and decisions he needed to make. She wanted to be supportive, but wasn't sure what to do.

So she didn't do anything.

She sat at her computer and stared at the screen saver until she heard him come back downstairs. She glanced at her watch, surprised to see that he'd been gone for half an hour. Then she looked up and saw him standing at the door with two suitcases in his hands. A sharp jolt of panic hit her, combined with an equally hard stab of fear.

"Are you going somewhere?" She forced out the words, her voice anything but firm.

He nodded. "I'm going back to the university. I can stay in my office until I figure out what to do about a place to live."

Vicki rose from her chair, her legs trembling so much she needed to hang on to the edge of the table to keep from falling. Uncontrollable shivers raced through her body. "But why?"

"Why?" He seemed genuinely surprised by her question. "I thought that would have been obvious. Planning for the future, that's what's most important to you. It seems to be the criteria by which you judge everything. A solid job, hard work, a well-planned future." His words became tinged with a hint of sarcasm bordering on bitterness, but not enough to hide the underlying despair and pain.

She stared at him, her mouth open but unable to force out any words.

"So, I'm returning to my job. If I work hard, perhaps I'll be able to measure up to your standards, to eventually become acceptable and be the type of person who will fit into your neatly ordered, planned out life." A sigh of resignation escaped his throat. "All I can do is try to be what you want."

He gave her a moment of eye contact before

turning and walking out the door.

Vicki heard his car start, then drive away. She went numb. Any form of logical thought eluded her. Nothing in her line of sight came into focus. She wasn't even sure she was still breathing. She had never felt so alone...or so lonely. She closed her eyes in an attempt to prevent the tears from flowing, but it didn't help. The moisture leaked out anyway and trickled down her cheeks. The cat, as if sensing its owner's inner turmoil, jumped up on the table and rubbed its head against her arm. Her feet had turned to lead, preventing her from moving.

Wave after wave of unbearable pain surged through her veins. Not one corner of her reality remained untouched. All she wanted to do was lock herself away and cry until she had no more tears. The perfect man for her had just walked out the door.

Correction—she had chased him away.

****

Blake unpacked his suitcases and put his clothes away as best he could in the limited amount of space. As a department head, his office included a small back room with sleeper sofa and a bathroom with a shower. It wasn't much, but it would do until he figured out his next move. He already had a lot of work piled on his desk. He wouldn't be teaching any classes until fall, but there were many things that needed to be accomplished before the term started. That included hiring an additional faculty member and filling two staff positions.

Part of him had to admit he missed the job he used to enjoy. But another part didn't want to answer questions or give explanations to his fellow faculty members. And then there was the part that wanted to be back at the beach with Vicki in his arms, recapturing the only truly enjoyable and carefree time he'd experienced since the death of his son. A time when he'd started to believe the future might hold something for him after all.

But now he didn't know what he felt other than numb and empty. When he'd lost Bobby, there wasn't anything he could do to bring his son back. Vicki, however, was a different situation. She was very much alive, and he loved her dearly. Could he be what she wanted? Could he fit into the mold of the type of man she deemed acceptable? He didn't know, but he had to try.

"Hey, Blake." A middle aged man with graying hair stuck his head in the door. "Good to see you back."

"Thanks, Charlie. From the look of these files, I have a lot of catching up to do. How are Helen and the boys?"

An amused chuckle escaped his friend's throat. "Summer has just started, and I'm already wondering when they'll be going back to school." Charlie glanced at his watch. "I've got to run. I have a class to teach. See you at the meeting Wednesday morning."

The rest of the day dragged by. More people stopped by his office to welcome him back. He hid behind a friendly, out-going façade, all the while wishing everyone would leave him alone. *Let me wallow in my misery.* He immediately admonished himself for the unacceptable and stupid thought. Self-pity was not the answer. He had spent two years grieving for his son and wallowing in his pain, a process he didn't intend to start over again, especially for someone very much alive. Somehow he had to get himself sorted out.

The halls finally quieted down. He locked his office door and retreated to the small back room. After watching the nightly news, he fell into a restless sleep. Dreams—no, more like memories—swirled through his mind. Vicki sleeping in his arms. Her face flushed from her orgasm. Sitting across the breakfast table from him. Next to him on the deck having a glass of wine in the evening and enjoying the sunset. Her excitement the first time she flew the kite. Every minute of the time they'd spent together, everything they shared.

Blake woke from his troubled sleep early the next morning, showered, dressed, and walked the few blocks to a coffee shop for breakfast. All he could manage was a few bites of an omelet and a cup of coffee. He didn't return to his office right away. Instead, he walked around the campus, stopping by the reflecting pond and strolling through the flower gardens. He had always loved the university grounds. The place had an energetic feel that invigorated him and fed into his overall sense of contentment. At least, it used to. He scanned the beautiful landscaping and stately old buildings amid the modern ones. Would he ever be able to recapture that special feeling?

And more importantly, would he be able to work out his relationship with Vicki?

He finally returned to his office and set up a schedule for the rest of the week. The first thing was a department head meeting at ten o'clock the next morning. He disliked the monthly meetings. They usually consisted of going over the same old things again and seldom accomplishing anything new, but they were a part of the job.

The rest of his day dragged by as slowly as the previous afternoon. No matter how hard he tried, he couldn't keep Vicki out of his thoughts. He loved her. Somehow he had to prove himself to her, show her he could be the type of man to fit into what she wanted out of life. But what about his own needs? He couldn't be so focused on pleasing Vicki that he ended up losing himself again. Somehow he had to figure out how to handle both dynamics.

He slowly shook his head as he sucked in a steadying breath. Was that even possible?

Chapter Ten

Vicki managed to pull herself out of bed on Wednesday morning. She made coffee, fed the cat, and thought about breakfast. Unable to face the idea of food, she went to work in her office. A couple of hours later, she finally gave up trying to concentrate. All she could think about was Blake Callahan...the man she loved. The man she had stupidly managed to drive away with her unreasonable obsessions and impractical vision of life. The man she desperately wanted back.

She had never been so angry with herself or so ashamed of her actions. It had been mid-morning on Monday when Blake had walked out the door with his suitcases. Forty-eight hours ago. The most miserable forty-eight hours of her life. She had hoped he would call, but was disappointed rather than surprised that he hadn't.

He'd trusted her with knowledge of the inner turmoil that had torn his life apart. And what had she done in return? She'd latched on to the fact that he had an impressive educational background with a good job and berated him for walking away from it. She could only guess how deeply she must have hurt him. And to have done it on top of the fact that he still grieved for his son. She had never thought of herself as being cruel, insensitive, or callous, but she didn't know how else to describe her deplorable actions and words even though she had never intended to hurt him.

She grabbed her coffee cup, took it out to the deck, and sat at the table. A beautiful sunny day. The type of day to be enjoyed. When she closed her eyes, an image popped into her mind. Blake flying one of his kites. The look of pleasure and fun covering his face. The excitement and enthusiasm his actions conveyed.

Vicki sat bolt upright, her eyes wide open. A rush of excitement hit her. The answer to her dilemma had been right in front of her all along. Grabbing her purse, she walked into the village. After making a quick purchase, she caught the bus. Forty-five minutes later, after transferring to another bus, she got off at the bus stop in front of the university's main entrance. She checked the campus map, then headed for the building housing the office of the head of the Sociology Department.

The doorknob turned, and the unlocked office door swung open. She wasn't sure whether she experienced relief or disappointment when she found the office empty. She placed the package on Blake's desk along with a sealed envelope. Nervous energy jittered inside her. She didn't know if she was doing the right thing, but she didn't know what else to do. Should she wait for him? No, his response to her note and gift had to be an honest one, not something prompted by her presence.

She retraced her bus route back to the village and walked to the house. Now the torturous reality of waiting. And time seemed to be at a standstill. Would he ignore her note? Would he call? Would he come home? Home... The sound of that word was very enticing. A home with the man she loved. An unlimited future that also included a marvelous *now*. A *today* she accepted as being every bit as important as tomorrow. The perfect balance. It had always been there, but she hadn't recognized it until Blake forced her to see it.

A quick glance into her office confirmed what she already knew. No way could she concentrate on work. After pouring herself a glass of iced tea, she took it out onto the deck. It was a beautiful day, the kind that seemed perfect for taking a walk along the beach. But she didn't dare leave. She couldn't take a chance on missing Blake's call.

If he called.

One hour gone. Then two hours. Apprehension welled inside her, so much so that her anxiety had become almost palpable. Had her actions been too little, too late? Had he chosen to ignore her note? It would soon be dinner time, and she hadn't eaten anything all day. She tried to stand, but her muscles refused to comply. It was as if her body had been drained of all energy, as if she had no reason to go on. Picking up her glass, she took the last swallow.

The sound of the glass door sliding open behind her grabbed her attention. The breath caught in her lungs. She closed her eyes in an attempt to compose herself. Had she really heard the sound, or had she only wanted it to be true so much that she had imagined it?

"May I join you?" Blake's voice caused unfettered joy to swell inside her heart.

She slowly turned. "Yes, I'd like that."

His face looked a little drawn. His eyes said he hadn't been sleeping well. But in spite of that, she'd never seen anything as wonderful.

Blake took a deep breath, held it a second, and then

slowly exhaled. Hesitantly at first, then with a fervor that couldn't be stopped, he pulled her up from the chair and folded her in his embrace. He held her closely, his cheek resting against her head. She wrapped her arms around his waist. It had only been two days, but it felt like a lifetime since he'd last held her.

"Thank you for my present. It's exactly the kind of kite I've been thinking about buying."

"I know. The store owner is one of my clients. He said you'd looked at it a couple of times as if you couldn't quite make up your mind."

"The envelope you left me…are you serious? You really filled out an entry form for the adult beginner classification of the kite flying contest?"

"Yes. The more I thought about what you said, the more it sounded like a fun thing to do. Of course, I'll need a lot of help and practice. I was hoping I could talk you into coaching me."

"You didn't do that because you thought I wanted you to, did you?" He wrinkled his brow into a frown. "I don't want you to enter the contest unless *you* want to. Nothing is fun when you're doing it because you feel like you have to, that it's expected of you rather than doing it because it's something you really want to do."

"I really want to." She brushed a soft kiss across his lips. "And what about going back to the university? I don't want you to do that unless it's something *you* want to do."

"When I left here Monday morning, I did it because it was what you so clearly wanted." He paused, trying to collect the rest of his thoughts and put them into words. "Having a responsible job and working for the future was what you needed from me, the thing that would make me acceptable so I could be part of your life. But now that I've gotten back into the swing of things, I realize how much I missed it." He cupped her face in his hands and captured her mouth with a loving kiss. "And how much I missed you."

"I'm so sorry, Blake." She held him tighter. "I had no right to say anything about your decision to leave the university. It was none of my business. I was completely out of line." She looked up at him, making eye contact. "Please forgive my selfishness. My callousness in trying to fit everything into some stupid, preconceived mold of how I thought the world should be."

"There's nothing to forgive." Keeping hold of her hand, he led the way inside and up the stairs.

She noted the suitcases on the floor of his bedroom. "Does this mean you're home for real?"

"Home? I like the sound of that word." He undressed her as he continued to talk. "Yes, I'm home for real. And how about you? Would you be willing to consider this your home? Your *permanent* home?" The last of her clothes fell to the floor.

"My *permanent* home? Are you saying…"

He'd already started it. He had to finish. "I'm saying that Gary Sanderson is considering selling this house. I want to buy it, but only if you agree to share it with me permanently. I love you, Vicki. I want us to share our lives together."

"Are you sure?" Her words came out as a soft whisper. "This has all happened so suddenly, this intensity and connection between us."

"I've never been so sure of anything in my life. I love you. I love you so very much."

"I love you, too." She unbuttoned his shirt and ran her hands across his chest before circling her arms around him. "I think I started falling in love with you when you first kissed me. I didn't want it to be so, but I couldn't stop it from happening."

"Would you like to show me just how much love that might be?" A wickedly sexy little grin tugged at the corners of his mouth.

She lowered the zipper on his slacks and reached in to fondle his balls through his briefs, then stroked his growing erection. She flashed him a sexy smile of her own. "That depends. Do you have any more of that chocolate body paint hidden away?"

"I can find the body paint if you can find some whipped cream."

"Mmm, chocolate body paint, whipped cream, and love. Sounds like a tasty dessert." She slid her hand inside his briefs and wrapped it around the girth of his hard shaft.

"You're the tastiest dessert there is, Mrs. Vicki Callahan."

"Mrs. Callahan?" Had she heard him correctly? "Is that what you said?"

"I was trying it out to hear how it sounded, to make sure it felt comfortable."

"And?" She held her breath awaiting his response.

"It sounds right. In fact, it sounds perfect. Since we're going to be living together, perhaps we should make it legal. Is that okay with you?"

"Those are definitely the most glorious words I've ever heard."

"So…is that a *yes* to my marriage proposal?"

"You bet it is."

Blake quickly discarded his clothes and pulled her into bed with him. "Let's take the other bedroom and turn it into your office. That way we can have our dining room back."

He didn't wait for her to answer. With the tip of his tongue, he traced the outline of the heart shaved on her mound. He flicked his tongue across her clit, then sucked it into his mouth. Her body writhed beneath him. Her soft moans turned into cries of delight.

"I love you, Blake. Oh, God...I love you so much."

Orgasmic waves crashed through Vicki. Her pussy tried to grab his tongue. Every place he touched her, even with the slightest caress, sent her into convulsive tremors. Her entire body quivered as the rapture claimed her. She wanted more of him. She wanted to pleasure him as he had her. Evening turned to night. Heated sex turned to tender lovemaking. Lovemaking that came from a true love.

A love for today and tomorrow.

About the Author

Samantha Gentry currently lives in Kansas but has lived most of her life in the Los Angeles area.

For twenty years she worked in television production before becoming a full time writer. For many years photography was her avocation, and that's what started her writing—non-fiction magazine articles to accompany her photographs. The writing eventually segued into fiction and novels.

To learn more about Samantha Gentry and her books, take a look at her website and check out her blog.

Visit Samantha at
www.samanthagentry.com
http://samanthagentry.blogspot.com

To chat with Samantha Gentry and other Wild Rose Press authors of erotic romance, join us at www.groups.yahoo.com/group/thewilderroses.

Also Available

Island Encounter
by
Samantha Gentry

He wants revenge. She wants peace.

A man with the wealth and power to make things happen, Flynn Ormond is about to see his decade-long quest for revenge fulfilled. But then he stumbles onto a bikini-clad beauty sunbathing on his deserted beach. He wants her, and he's accustomed to getting what he wants. However, she's a distraction he can't afford, not at all what she seems, and stands against everything he believes is right.

Traci Meredith has a long term plan of her own, to confront the man responsible for the death of her parents and finally move on with her life. But when sun-kissed god of a caretaker wanders into her life one sunny morning, she lets more than the tropical paradise seduce her from her goal. Then she discovers the truth of his identity and the length he'll go to for justice. Can she lure him from destruction's grip or will the fingers of the past hold on tight?

Also Read

Sin City Alibi
by
Sophia Ryan

http://amzn.com/B014JLZ11I

Sometimes what happens in Vegas follows you home.
Jumping libido-first into a cliché Vegas fling is the last thing on Dani Parker's mind when she flies to Sin City for some R&R after her lover/boss, Elliott, dumps her. But an innocent night of flirty fun with a sexy hunk she knows only as Matt whirlwinds into a sinfully hot weekend. Back home, she discovers her boss has been murdered, her Vegas fling is heading the investigation into financial irregularities for the company she works for, and she's smack-dab in the middle of both.

Matt Collins has filled his life with work and no-strings sex since the day his heart went on lock-down. No woman ever cracked that lock. Until Dani. Now all he wants is her in his bed and in his life, but the odds for success are stacked against him. She can't accept his conditions for love, there's evidence suggesting she and her former lover embezzled from the company, and the cops arrest her for Elliott's murder. His gut tells him she's innocent and he wasn't just an alibi, but his heart remembers the brutal past that still haunts him.

When everything Matt and Dani hold dear is on the line, they'll learn that sometimes risking everything leads to the most satisfying payouts.

Thank you for purchasing this
publication of The Wild Rose Press, Inc.
If you enjoyed the story, we would appreciate
your letting others know by leaving a review.
For other wonderful stories, please visit our
on-line bookstore at www.wilderroses.com.

For questions or more
information contact us at
info@thewildrosepress.com.

The Wild Rose Press, Inc.
www.thewilderroses.com

Stay current with The Wild Rose Press, Inc.
Like us on Facebook
https://www.facebook.com/TheWildRosePress
And Follow us on Twitter
https://twitter.com/WildRosePress